Ultimate Justice

M. A. COMLEY

ISBN-13: 978-1505646450

ISBN-10: 1505646456

OTHER BOOKS BY
NEW YORK TIMES BEST SELLING AUTHOR
M. A. COMLEY

Cruel Justice

Impeding Justice

Final Justice

Foul Justice

Guaranteed Justice

Ultimate Justice

Virtual Justice

Hostile Justice

Tortured Justice

Rough Justice (coming Jan 2015)

Blind Justice (A Justice novella)

Evil In Disguise (Based on true events)

Forever Watching You (#1 D I Miranda Carr Thrillers)

Torn Apart (Hero Series #1)

End Result (Hero Series #2)

Sole Intention (Intention Series #1)

Grave Intention (Intention Series #2)

It's A Dog's Life (A Lorne Simpkins short story)

ACKNOWLEDGMENTS

As always love and best wishes to my wonderful Mum for the role she plays in my career. Special thanks to my superb editor Stefanie, and my wonderful cover artist Karri. Thanks also to Joseph my amazing proof reader.

Licence Notes.

Ultimate Justice

Prologue

The swell of the sea had doubled in size in the last thirty minutes.

"Skipper, it's no good. We won't make it," Taylor shouted above the thunder and the howling wind that surrounded them.

The captain threw back his right arm, which connected hard with Taylor's face. Taylor staggered unsteadily on his feet and landed heavily against the door to the tiny bridge. "Get away from me, you imbecile. I give the orders around here, not you. You hear me?"

Taylor righted himself and surged forward, determined to make the captain change his mind. It would be foolish for them to try to enter the port in a storm like this. He watched out the starboard porthole at the waves continually bombarding the deck, and knew they wouldn't have long before the sea welcomed them with open arms and sucked the life out of them. Thoughts of his wife, Sonia, and his three adorable children entered his mind and stayed there, as if mocking him for undertaking this perilous voyage, despite the huge risk involved. Unexpectedly, his family's beautiful smiles and the shocking thought that he'd never see any of them again spurred him into action.

He scanned the wheelhouse for a possible weapon. He saw a metal bar in the corner and pounced on it. "Skipper, stand away from the helm."

Captain Smythe, a man built like a heavy weight boxer, snarled at Taylor before his gaze drifted to the bar he was holding. "Think you can take me on, sonny? Fancy a bit of mutiny, do ya?"

"Our lives are in danger, Skipper. Surely you can see that?" Taylor watched as madness seemed to settle in his aggressor's eyes.

"I see no such thing. It's a storm, and a tiny one at that. I've been at sea longer than you've been out of nappies, lad. Now, let me bring this old girl and her cargo in. Have a day off from your foolishness for a change. Leave this job for a real man to handle."

The captain's undermining of him incensed Taylor. He gritted his teeth and his knuckles turned white around the bar he was holding. Smythe turned his attention back to fighting the helm. "You fucking idiot." Taylor ran at him, screaming like a banshee with the bar high above his head. "I'll be damned if I'll stand by and let you kill us all."

Smythe cried out in pain as the bar crashed against his skull, but he didn't go down as Taylor had expected. "Ya bastard. Think you can take me on, do ya? You're the fucking idiot around here if you think that." Smythe's iron-like hands connected with first the right and then the left side of Taylor's face, leaving him dazed. The bar crashed to the floor, and stunned, Taylor held his head in his hands. He'd never been hit so hard by a man before, and he'd been in several fights over his thirty-odd years on Earth.

The boat swayed violently as both men stood their ground, eyeing each other with caution and contempt, but at the same time unaware of the screams coming from the hold below.

The captain beckoned to Taylor. "Come on, then, if you think you're hard enough. Give me what you've got, you nancy boy, with your snooty redheaded wife and your two point four children."

The captain's intentional goading worked, and Taylor charged him with all his might. The captain's chest puffed out and his fists clenched into tight balls. Taylor was clobbered around both ears before he got within a foot of Smythe, but he kept up his charge, despite being almost knocked senseless. Taylor bowed his head low and charged into the captain's portly stomach. Smythe only laughed at his inept attempt to bring him down.

Taylor, his blood boiling with anger, stooped to the floor and retrieved the bar. He swung it like a golf club at the captain's lower leg. With the boat being tossed in the high waves, the captain lost his balance and hollered as he went down. His head hit the side of the binnacle supporting the helm, and blood erupted from a wound above his right eye. Taylor tried to stop the wheel from spinning out of control, catching his hand several times in the spokes in the process. "Fuck!" he cried out as a bone snapped in his little finger.

The captain, who was lying on the floor, laughed.

Taylor glared at him, then turned his attention back to the helm, and, watching it intently, he waited for the opportune moment to come his way. Finally, he grabbed one of the spokes firmly with both hands while he anchored himself behind the wheel, his feet spread wide apart. Feeling calmer now that he appeared to have the vessel under control, he guided the ship out to sea and away from the port they had been heading towards.

"Turn this ship around. If you don't, we'll go under for sure," the captain insisted.

"Shut your mouth. If I'd left things for you to sort out, we would have been smashed to pieces on the rocks by now."

"It takes decades of experienced sailing to become a captain. You've got neither the balls nor the stamina, sonny, to bring this ship home safely."

"We'll see about that, old man." Taylor focused fully on the task at hand and chose to ignore anything else the captain had to say. In the distance, he could hear the ghostly screams of their cargo riding on the howling wind. He gulped down the frustration building within him and steered the vessel through the tumultuous waves. Out of the corner of his eye, he saw the captain struggle to his feet. But there was little Taylor could do about the captain's impending attack. His back took the force of the captain's strike. He gasped for breath as the air was driven from his lungs. Excruciating pain shot through his body.

"Take that, you bastard. I'm taking control of my ship. *My* ship, you hear me?" The captain ran to the wheel.

Taylor's hand went in search of what was causing the pain in his back, and his heart sank when he discovered the six-inch blade embedded there. He crumpled to his knees as the blood started to drain from his body. The beautiful faces of his young family flashed before his eyes once again. He asked only one thing: "Why?"

The captain took his eye off the sea for a split second to glance at Taylor, and that was when disaster struck. The wheel spun out of Smythe's hand, and the force sent him reeling across to the other side of the bridge. The whole boat lurched sideways and water flooded through the open bulkhead door as it flew open. With his life slipping away, Taylor didn't have the strength to stop himself from being swept out the doorway and onto the deck.

Smythe did nothing to prevent his exit for, despite his hulking frame, the water dragged the captain through the doorway after Taylor. They both choked on the salt water as the mighty energy of the unforgiving, raging sea pulled their heads under the surface. Taylor watched his captain resurface three or four times, his body smashing against the taffrail a few times before being washed overboard and out to sea. Taylor finally succumbed to the sea's beckoning call.

It wasn't long before the ship, in her last death throes, finally sank.

The sea sighed with satisfaction at the devastation it had caused, yet no one was there to hear it. Even the ship's valuable cargo had been silenced.

CHAPTER ONE

"Why, you little monkey, bite the hand that feeds you, would you?" Lorne picked up the bundle of black and white fluff and kissed the eight-week-old pup on the tip of his nose.

"He'll soon learn that you don't take crap from men," Tony laughed before he took a sip of his coffee.

"Hey, you cheeky sod, who asked you for your opinion? Aren't they just adorable?" Lorne placed the male pup back in the zoned-off area in the kitchen with his six siblings and then fluttered her eyelashes innocently at her husband.

Tony replied with two simple words: "Yes. No."

"What do you mean, 'no?'"

Tony laughed and shook his head. "I was pre-empting your next question," he told her. Then he put on a whiny voice and continued, "Couldn't we make room in the house for just one more dog? Henry's lonely."

Lorne rose from the floor, picked the tea towel up off the counter, and aimed it at his head. "Dear husband of mine, has anyone ever told you that you can be cuttingly mean at times?"

Tony reached out and pulled her onto his lap, kissing her hard on the lips. The kiss took her breath away for a second or two. He murmured against her lips, "Umm…yes—you. But I tend to ignore what you say half the time."

A cough from the doorway interrupted their romantic moment. Lorne's father, Sam Collins, looked embarrassed as he walked over to the kettle and switched it on. "Don't mind me, you two."

Lorne shot off Tony's lap and went to hug her father. "Sorry, Dad. I didn't know you were up. Did you sleep all right?"

Her father pecked her on the cheek. "Not really, love. I was awake for three or four hours during the night, as usual."

Lorne had been worried about her father's insomnia for months now. Since he'd been hospitalised with meningitis, his sleep had been dramatically affected. In turn, this had hampered his ability to lend a hand around the rescue centre. It was like a domino effect in that this also hindered Lorne's new private investigation business. But there was a light at the end of that particularly dark tunnel, as the school holidays were just around the corner. Which meant that

Charlie, Lorne's teenage daughter, would be eager to help out more around the kennels, tending to the numerous strays Lorne was trying—without much luck—to rehome. Due to the recession hitting the UK, their occupancy numbers had risen to an all-time high of thirty. Ever the softie where dogs were concerned, Lorne found it exceedingly difficult to turn away animals in need, hence the little family of pups invading her family's private space. The only member of the family who didn't seem to mind the pups being there was their Border collie, Henry. The devoted collie kept a constant watch over the tiny pups as if they were his own flesh and blood.

Concerned, Lorne hooked her arm through her father's. "Why don't you go back to bed, Dad? We can handle things around here this morning."

Unhooking his arm, her father smiled. "I'll be fine. When you get to my age—closer to the grave—you need less sleep, anyway."

"Dad, what a dreadful thing to say." Lorne glanced over at Tony, hoping he would back her up and reprimand her father, but he didn't. As usual, he stayed out of their father–daughter discussions. Just as her father remained silent during those times when Lorne and Tony's marital bliss wasn't so blissful. Not that they argued much—any arguments Lorne and Tony had were miniscule compared to the ones she'd had with Charlie's father, Tom.

"I'm only being honest, love. It's something you're going to have to get used to. I'll be joining your mum soon enough." Tears misted Lorne's eyes, and her father hugged her. "You, daft mare. Don't go getting all maudlin on me. Hey, where's my breakfast? I fancy scrambled eggs on toast this morning. Have you two eaten?"

Lorne knew that was her cue to back off. Her father was an expert at changing conversations midway through when the subject matter got too tough to handle.

"We had some toast earlier. You sit down and I'll do it for you, Dad." His expression reprimanded her without him having to open his mouth. She held up her hands in submission. "Okay, I'll get the eggs out of the pantry for you. I collected them this morning from the hens. I was wondering whether we should put a small table out the front with an honesty box—what do you think?"

"Sure, if you want the front of the house pelted with eggs," Tony muttered as he picked up the morning paper.

"You're such a misanthropist, Mr. Former MI6 Agent."

"Umm...rightly so, if you've read any of the papers lately. I wouldn't trust the youth of today to pick their noses right, let alone do anything else correctly."

"Yuck, Tony! You know what? You sound like an old man. Wait a minute—are you including Charlie in that sweeping generalisation?"

Tony winced as if he'd received a sucker punch to his gut from an invisible man. "Damn, I forgot about Charlie."

Lorne's father was beating his eggs with a fork. "It would take some doing to forget about *that* one."

"Wow! You two are unbelievable. She'll be helping out more around here during the summer break. I hope you'll both try to at least give her a chance."

"I'm joking. Anyway, I'm sure Tony didn't mean to tar her with the same brush as the other hoodlums around today. What was it my old granddad used to say, now? Oh yes: 'there are always exceptions to the rule.' After what that girl has been through over the years, she's had to grow up faster than any other kid her age. She's mature beyond her years, which will stand her in good stead in the future."

Lorne nodded, but deep down in her gut, the old pangs of guilt started up. Charlie's childhood had been stripped from her at the hands of a man who had been Lorne's nemesis for years. She shuddered at the thought of what the Unicorn had done to Charlie almost four years ago.

"Stop that," Tony ordered, breaking through her dark reverie.

"What?" she pretended she didn't have a clue what her husband was talking about.

He raised a questioning eyebrow. "You know. I can tell when your thoughts turn to that lunatic and your guilt resurfaces. Stop it now. Tell her, Sam."

Her father put his breakfast on hold as the conversation became more serious. "Tony's right, love. You can't keep punishing yourself for what happened to Charlie. Take a leaf out of her book. She's accepted it and moved on."

Lorne spread her arms out and slapped her hands on her thighs. "I know you're both right, but it doesn't alter the fact that I still blame myself for involving my family in that case."

Sam gathered his daughter in his arms and cushioned her head against his chest. "You didn't. Baldwin involved Charlie, *not* you."

"I know, Dad. I try not to think of it, but sometimes—just sometimes—it catches me out."

Sam pushed her away from him and tucked a loose lock of hair behind her ear, like he used to do when she was a child. "It's bound to, love. Events of that awful day—those few days—changed all of our lives. Look at it this way: if that day hadn't happened, then you and Tony would never have met."

Tony snorted. "Any chance I can turn the clock back four years to before that day?"

Lorne flew out of her father's arms and clipped Tony around the head. "You cheeky sod. I'll get my own back, just you wait and see."

Tony held his hand out horizontally in front of him. "Look, steady as a rock. You don't scare me, Mrs. Former Detective Inspector."

"Huh, we'll see," Lorne retorted. She let the idle threat linger between them for a while before she spoke again. "I hope the weather is better than yesterday's. That storm caused havoc to the roads across the country. There were flashfloods in several areas, apparently."

Tony picked up his paper again. "How typically British of you, Lorne, to change the subject to the weather like that."

"A trick I picked up from you, I believe, dear hubby."

Her father settled himself into the chair next to Lorne and started eating his breakfast. Lorne watched, grateful that his appetite hadn't been affected by his illness like his sleep had. After swallowing a mouthful of bacon, he said, "That was one of the worst storms we'd had in years. I still laugh when I think of weatherman Bill Giles ending up with egg on his face when he totally ignored a viewer's comment about a hurricane brewing back in '86. If I recall rightly, Seven Oaks almost had to change its name to 'One Oak' after it got battered by a storm."

"Yes. The UK didn't cope well with the conditions around that time. The railways came to a virtual standstill and most of the small country roads became impassable, if I remember rightly," Tony said, looking thoughtful before he continued, "Thankfully, I was oversees at the time, on holiday with my parents in Crete."

"Lucky you! The farthest we went when we were kids was to Butlins at Minehead." Lorne sniggered.

"It took a lot to run that old house of ours. Your mother always liked to have nice new furniture every five years or so, something had to give. I'm afraid Minehead was all we could afford back then, love. Mind you, I reckon that nowadays it's just as cheap to go abroad as to spend a week at a holiday camp in the UK," her father replied. A sad little smile had settled on his face when he'd mentioned Lorne's mother. It had been a struggle for him to get over her death from breast cancer. He hadn't really shown signs of wanting to go on with his own life until Lorne and Tony had bought the rescue centre and asked him to live with them. It was as though they'd given him a new purpose in life.

Lorne smiled to reassure him. "It's all right, Dad, you don't have to justify anything. I loved the holidays we went on when we were kids. With you working long hours on the force, any time Jade and I had with you was special to us."

"What the heck?" Tony angled the paper so his wife could see the article that had caught his eye.

"What's that?" Lorne's father asked.

Lorne shook her head as she read and then glanced up at her father. "It's terrible. A boat capsized off the Kent coastline yesterday. It says here that details are still a little sketchy, but apparently the boat was carrying some kind of human cargo."

"No! Human trafficking, you mean?"

"That's how I'm reading it. What's your take on it, Tony?"

Tony hitched his right shoulder up and his mouth tugged down at the sides. "It's hard to say without actually knowing what the authorities have found."

Lorne left the table and went in search of her laptop. She returned and booted it up. "Let's see what was reported on the news last night, shall we?"

After locating a video clip that had appeared on Sky news the previous evening, they watched in silence as a windswept journalist, standing on a pebbled beach in Kent, told the viewers that rescuers were still recovering bodies from the shipwreck. "So far, at least twenty-five people of Asian origin—all dead—have been recovered." The camera panned over his shoulder and there, lying on the beach, was a row of bodies covered in tarpaulin sheets. The camera swung out to sea, focusing on an incoming dinghy that had two men in wetsuits on board. Several men on the shoreline awaited their arrival. When the dinghy was pulled ashore, another dead body was lifted out of the boat and gently placed alongside the others.

Lorne's eyes moistened. "That's awful, just awful. Those poor people. Do they know how big the boat was?"

Tony looked back at the paper and quickly scanned the article again. "It doesn't say. But if it hit the rocks, it would have been busted up pretty badly. I doubt they'll be able to tell what size vessel it was for a while, unless they find out the name of it."

Lorne stared at the wall in front of her as she imagined Charlie's dead body lying on the beach. She shook her head ridding her mind of the unwanted image. "Am I being overly sensitive about this, you guys? Or is this story too sad for words?"

Both Tony and her father looked at her, but it was Tony who answered first, "Maybe you are being a touch sensitive about it, but that's you, babe. You care what happens to people. Old wounds are bound to resurface when stories like this hit the headlines."

"That's probably it," her father agreed. "The similarities to what Charlie went through—that's what is affecting you. That's my guess, anyway."

"You could be right, Dad. I've just got a feeling here," she placed her hand across her stomach and winced as if she was in pain. "Something is pushing me to delve deeper into this case. Is that daft?"

Tony rose from the table and walked over to her. "I'd say there was something wrong with you if you *didn't* want to look further into this, Lorne. But sweetheart, we've got to stop doing *pro bono* cases. Unless someone comes forward asking us to investigate the case, we're going to have to let this one pass us by."

Lorne dipped her head and rested it on Tony's chest. Her husband was right—of course he was. She glanced over at her father and smiled. His eyes rose to the ceiling before he continued to eat his breakfast. He knew her so well, well enough to know that she would grab the case if the slightest opportunity came her way. Especially as the private eye side of things was relatively slow at the moment.

"Okay, I'm tired of all this maudlin news. What's on the agenda for today?" Tony planted a tender kiss on her forehead and then pushed her away from him.

"The usual, I guess. Cleaning out the kennels and feeding the hounds. I do have to make a home visit this afternoon, though. Could you both spare me for an hour or two?"

Tony tutted and sighed heavily. "If we must."

Lorne playfully punched him in the stomach. "That's twice I'll need to get my own back now."

They all laughed, and Lorne reached over to turn off the depressing news channel and put on ITV's Daybreak, instead. She cringed when the presenter introduced a celebrity Lorne strongly disliked. She strode over to the back door. "Think I'd rather clean up dog poo than listen to what that idiot has to say."

Tony laughed and followed her out. "I think I would, too."

For the next hour, the husband and wife team messed around in the kennels, cleaning and playing with the permanent inmates before they moved over to the new kennel block, which housed the temporary boarders whose owners were enjoying themselves on holiday.

At eleven o'clock that morning Tony began going through the list of repairs he had to carry out, and Lorne headed inside to start on some paperwork.

After a quick bite to eat at lunchtime, Lorne jumped in her father's Nova and drove to Natasha Wallace's elegant house in the country.

CHAPTER TWO

Lorne approached the Wallaces' mansion for the second time in as many months. It never ceased to amaze her how the other half lived. It rankled her that the rich seemed to flaunt their wealth so arrogantly when there were so many starving people in the world who could benefit from the loose change in their pockets. She knew that Natasha Wallace sat on the boards of several well-known charities both at home and abroad, and did her very best to aid those in desperate need, but Lorne wished that more rich people were as philanthropic as Bill Gates.

The gardener tending the circular rose bed in front of the house tipped his hat as she passed him. Lorne drew to a halt and pressed the button to lower the passenger's side window in order to talk to him. "The garden is looking gorgeous, Frank. You're doing an excellent job."

"Why, thank you, miss. The lady of the house is around the back with that little minx of a dog. Bloomin' thing got in the walled garden the other day and dug up some of me carrots."

Lorne's face flushed with embarrassment, she'd always regarded the dog as well-behaved when he was with her. "Oops, sorry about that. Hope they weren't damaged too much."

He waved a hand in front of him. "Nah, not really. He's a real cutie, that one. I quite often wonder if Mrs. Wallace would miss him if I tucked the little fellow in my pocket and took him home to the missus."

"By all accounts, Mrs. Wallace has become very attached to the little chap. I'm sure she would miss him terribly if you did that."

"That she would, miss, that she would. Have a pleasant visit."

Lorne smiled, pushed the button to put the window back up, and continued her drive up the crunching gravelled driveway. She parked the car at the front and stepped onto the narrow path that ran along the side of the property and led to the pool area at the back. The view momentarily took Lorne's breath away as she walked through the wooden arch which was covered by fragrantly scented pink and white roses. The garden expanded into an abundance of late spring-early summer colour. Lorne suspected the garden was around two acres or thereabouts, but the extended view of the green fields beyond added to the garden's width and length.

"Lorne! Over here."

She waved at Natasha and slowly made her way over to the pool area, which was surrounded by a variety of assorted coloured lavenders. She could hear the bees contentedly working their way through their nectar. Several butterflies took flight as the lavender brushed against her calf. The place had a magical and calming effect that made Lorne let out a satisfied sigh. *Ah, how the other half live!*

She could hear the yapping of the Pekingese before she saw the tiny dog. "I see he's settled in well." At the sound of her voice, the dog left Natasha's side and ran up to Lorne. She scooped up the white dog, which resembled a powder puff, into her arms and kissed the excited creature on the nose. "Tiny, you're still as adorable as ever."

Natasha cleared her throat and hesitantly stated, "Umm…we had a little name change. He's called Timmy now. Although he should be called 'Terror,' the amount of mischief he gets into."

Lorne laughed and set the dog down on the limestone slabs that surrounded the pool. He trotted back to his owner with his tail erect and wagging he ran under the lounger and into his round sheepskin bed. "The name suits him. Frank filled me in on what the little toe-rag has been up to. He seems happy here, Mrs. Wallace."

"Come now, call me Natasha. Yes, he's so sweet. Sometimes I have to stop myself from cuddling the life out of him."

"I'm so pleased he's found another loving home. His previous owner still rings me every other day to see how he is. It's a shame these care homes don't allow the residents to keep their pets with them."

"It is a great shame. Maybe I'll go and visit the lady someday to show her how Timmy is doing."

Lorne could tell Natasha was just saying that to be kind and that she had no real intention of doing any such thing. She really couldn't see Natasha being caught dead in a council-run care home—or any other care home, for that matter.

In the distance, Lorne could hear the slight clinking sound of crockery. She looked over her shoulder and saw a maid approaching them carrying a tray with teacups, saucers, and a bone china teapot. The young woman set the tray down on the table and walked away. Lorne thought it was strange that the girl hadn't acknowledged her existence at all. No sideways glance, nothing.

Natasha must have noticed the way Lorne was looking at the maid, because as soon as the girl had moved out of earshot, she said, "I apologise for Mai Lin."

"What do you mean?"

"She's usually a smiley little thing with impeccable manners. Unfortunately, she received a call last night from a relative with some sad news."

Lorne didn't really want to intrude into the maid's personal business, but something intrigued her enough to ask. "Sad news? Did she say what?"

Natasha looked taken aback for a second or two, but then she shrugged. "I can't see what harm it will do to tell you. It was in that ghastly storm yesterday. Mai Lin suspects her younger sister was in an accident."

"An accident? What accident?" Lorne asked. Distractedly, she poured the tea into the two cups and handed one to Natasha.

Natasha swung her legs off the lounger and onto the ground. She took the cup from Lorne and stared into the brown liquid as she recounted the phone call Mai Lin had received. "I suppose it was around eight last night when she received a frantic call from her mother back home in Bangkok. It only lasted a few minutes. She comes from a very poor family; her mother works for a wealthy businessman. He allows her to make the odd call if there is an emergency. Anyway, I digress: as soon as the call came, I sensed there was trouble. The colour instantly drained from Mai Lin's face as she took the call. Her mother said that she had been working and had seen on her boss's TV that a boat had been wrecked in the storm—"

Lorne gasped. "You mean she thinks her sister was on-board *that* boat—the boat on the news at the moment? My God, that poor girl! Poor Mai Lin."

"Her mother says she knows deep down her daughter was on that boat. You know what a mother's instinct can be like? Isn't it dreadful? Her sister was coming here for a better life. I knew nothing about it until last night. I've asked Mai Lin what I can do to help, but she says nothing. She'll deal with her loss in her own way. She's gone into her shell. She's always been a little timid, but now she just won't speak to me at all. I feel so inadequate."

"Grief affects people in different ways, Natasha. I wouldn't take it personally if I were you."

"Oh, I'm not. I just wish I could help the poor girl, that's all. But she keeps shutting me out."

"Cultural differences. I'm sure if she needs your help, she'll ask. Has she worked here long?"

"About a year now, I suppose. I doubt she'll ask for my help, though; she's never asked before. Bloody hell, I didn't even know her sister was coming to England."

"It does seem odd that she didn't tell you. Have you seen the news this morning?"

"No. I've tried to keep the TV off in case it upsets Mai Lin."

Lorne nodded her understanding, pulled out a chair, and sat down heavily on the wrought iron seat. "Well, I tracked the story down on my laptop this morning and immediately wished I hadn't." Lorne took a sip of tea before she continued, "The cameraman was filming when they pulled another body from the sea. The camera panned around, and there were numerous bodies on the shore. They were laid out side by side and covered with tarpaulin sheets. Even the hardest of hearts would have found that an upsetting sight. If Mai Lin had witnessed that, she would have been devastated. I know I was, and I didn't know any of the victims."

Natasha's hand flew up and covered her bikini-clad chest. "How truly awful. Who'd have thought a storm could cause such damage?"

"I take it from what you've told me already you have no idea how Mai Lin's sister obtained her ticket?"

Natasha shook her head. "Not a clue. I'm not sure she would tell me even if I asked. Why?"

Lorne smiled, but avoided the question. Thinking back to what Tony and her father had said at breakfast about the vessel probably being involved in human trafficking, she didn't want to cast any aspersions without the necessary proof. "Hey, are you in the market for rehoming another little dog, should one come in to the centre?"

As the conversation reverted back to Timmy, Natasha's smile broadened and she snapped her fingers to encourage the dog out from the shade under the lounger. Timmy joined them and sat in front of Natasha, begging for a treat. He jiggled his front paws up and down until he got one. "I'm not sure I could sweet-talk my hubby into having a second dog. He loves Timmy to bits, but I don't think men view dogs in the same way as us, do they? Why do you ask? Is there a new dog due in? Another old dear going into a home or something?"

"No, nothing like that. I can see that Timmy has landed on his feet here and is very comfortable in his surroundings; that isn't always the case when we rehome dogs. No matter how fussy I am on the home visits before I place a dog in a new home, one bad penny never fails to slip through the net. If I know a dog is well loved, then I always ask if the new owner would be willing to take on another dog. Saves me advertising costs, etc."

"That's understandable. Actually, a couple of the ladies I occasionally lunch with have taken your card. I'm not sure any of them would be interested in the larger dogs you are trying to rehome, but they all adore Timmy. I'm sure some of them will be in touch with you soon."

Lorne cringed inside, but kept the smile prominently fixed on her face. The last thing she wanted was a group of snooty women turning up at the centre looking for a tiny breed to keep their handbags warm. That was the kind of road she didn't intend going down. Laughing, she said, "I'm so glad you're not the type of woman who sees Timmy as a handbag dog. I can't abide it when these footballers' wives and girlfriends—WAGS, are they called?—display those poor creatures in their expensive Gucci handbags. If only they knew the psychological damage they are doing to the dogs. Sheila, the lady who got me involved in rescuing dogs, has told me quite a few horror stories about how the dogs start biting their owners; some of the poor mites even lose the use of their little legs because they're carried around everywhere."

"No! Really? Well, rest assured that Timmy won't ever be treated that way, Lorne. I'll be sure to put off any of my girlfriends who have ideas along those lines. What shameful behaviour. Chavs—that's what they are. Most of those girls have been pulled out of the gutter. Not the type I ever want to mix with. They stand out a mile at these functions I have to attend with Jason. You want to hear the bloody laughs on some of these girls. Really they are so uncouth it sends shivers up my spine just thinking about them. Horrid, *horrid* girls."

"I'm so glad we think along the same lines on this one, Natasha. If any of your friends get in touch do you mind if I ring you before I carry out a home visit?"

"Not at all. I'd be disappointed if you didn't." Natasha got up and moved her lithe, suntanned, glistening body over to the table. She picked up the brass bell sitting on its surface and rang it a few times. "Silly girl didn't bring any biscuits."

Lorne raised a hand. "Please don't bother on my account. I don't really like to eat between meals anyway."

"Well, I fancy a Ryvita. Love a crispbread at this time of day. I don't tend to eat lunch until about two or three o'clock. Jason likes to have his evening meal around nine. I'd never last if I ate at midday or one o'clock."

Mai Lin appeared and bowed in front of the table, and again Lorne noticed the way the girl totally avoided eye contact with her.

"Be a dear and bring me a crispbread with some cheese on, Mai Lin."

"Yes, ma'am. Sorry, ma'am," the maid said before she hurried back into the house. She returned within seconds carrying a second tray with a plate of crispbreads and a wedge of cheese on the side.

Lorne watched the girl's increasing discomfort around her. She tried to put the girl at ease by thanking her, despite the crispbreads being for Natasha and not for her, but yet again, the girl refused to make eye contact, Lorne couldn't help wondering why. She dipped forward to try to catch the girl's eye, and for the briefest moment, Mai Lin's gaze met hers. Lorne was shocked by the sadness she saw in her eyes, and by a noticeable discolouration that she had clearly tried to disguise with makeup underneath and around her eyes.

Hmm…that's strange. Maybe she's had a fall or something.

Natasha dismissed the girl, and she ran back into the house again under Lorne's watchful gaze.

Satisfied that Timmy had settled in to his new surroundings and that Natasha cared for him—despite feeling suddenly uncomfortable with how Mai Lin reacted to her visit—Lorne decided to leave.

"I'm glad Timmy has found his home for life, Natasha. Any problems at all, don't hesitate to ring me. I better get back home now, as I have a young family coming to pick out a dog early this afternoon."

"I understand, but it's a shame you can't stay and chat," Natasha said, nibbling on her crispbread.

As Lorne meandered back to the car, she couldn't help wondering if, in spite of her wealth, Natasha wasn't a very lonely woman. Lorne was distracted on the journey home, she thought a lot about Mai Lin's terrible situation. Having to deal with her sister's death in a strange country was one thing; however, Lorne was also concerned about the facial bruises Mai Lin had gone out of her way to try to cover up.

CHAPTER THREE

From the minute she arrived home until five o'clock, the afternoon proved to be chaotic. The centre was unusually busy with people dropping by wanting to offer some of the permanent boarders a new home, and the phone didn't stop ringing, either. Most of the calls had been enquiries from people wanting to board their dogs for a week or two's holiday, but sadly, they didn't have room for any more boarders. With all of them busy, in one way or another, Lorne didn't get the opportunity to voice her concerns about Mai Lin to either Tony or her father. Nonetheless, that didn't stop the girl's plight from popping into her mind now and then during the afternoon.

"Boy, what a day!" Tony announced, collapsing into one of the chairs around the kitchen table.

Lorne filled the kettle and turned to watch her tired father ease himself into the chair next to her husband. She tried to make light of how tired they all looked. "Huh! Men—no stamina for *real* work."

Tony was the first to pounce on her. "Says you. The one person who took time out to go off gallivanting."

"My sentiments exactly," her father added with a smirk.

"Ah, about that visit: I wanted to have a chat with both of you with regard to what happened during my visit. Let me make the coffee first." She glanced over her shoulder and watched the two men in her life exchange a puzzled look. After making the coffee, she placed a mug in front of everyone and sat down next to her husband.

"Come on, don't keep us waiting. We're not going to have to take the dog back, are we?"

"Not this time, no." Lorne blew on her coffee before she took a sip. It was a delay tactic while she mulled over how to tell them about Mai Lin's situation.

An impatient Tony asked, "What, then? Lorne, I know to be worried when you go quiet on us."

She smiled at her husband's exceptional perception. He really did know her well. "Okay. When I arrived at Natasha Wallace's house, everything with the dog went well. She's changed his name to Timmy and the little chap appears to be really happy there."

"So what's the problem?" her father piped up proving to be just as impatient as her husband.

"You two are incorrigible. Give me a chance, I'm getting there."

"Wish you'd speed it up a bit—I'm dying for a soak in the bath," Tony complained.

Lorne slapped the top of his arm and tutted. "Here's the thing: on my previous visit to Natasha's 'stately home,' I don't remember seeing a maid there."

"I'm not with you." Tony seemed confused.

"Give me a bloody chance, Tony. Right, so we were out by the pool, and the maid, a petite Asian girl, brought us out a tray of tea."

"So? What's unusual about that?" her father asked.

Frustrated that the two men kept interrupting her, she grabbed her mug and stood up, walked over to the worktop, and leaned her back against it so that she was still facing them. "Will you two just listen and stop interrupting me?" Both men nodded. "The girl seemed really upset, and after she left the tray and walked back into the house, I asked Natasha what was wrong with her. You'll never believe what she said."

"We're waiting," Tony replied.

"It turns out that Mai Lin's sister might have been aboard that boat on the news. You know, the one that went down in the storm."

"Wow!" Tony's exclamation hung between them for a second or two.

Lorne glanced at her father whose face had crinkled with concern. "Did you get a chance to ask her about why her sister might have been on the boat? Not that I think you'd get a straight answer if her sister was being trafficked."

"Precisely. I really didn't want to ask her all sorts of probing questions in front of Natasha. It wouldn't have been an appropriate time either considering she thinks her sister has just died. I'm not sure how to proceed. What do you guys suggest?"

Her father shrugged. "It's difficult, as we don't know the circumstances for her sister being aboard the boat, it could turn out to be completely innocent, although I doubt it. Only a fool or someone desperate would put themselves in jeopardy like that—cram themselves into a ship's hold on a long trip. We need to wait until we get all the information before getting involved."

"I agree," Tony said looking thoughtful. "Could you give Katy a call?"

"Good idea. It's her birthday on Sunday, and I was going to invite her to spend the weekend with us anyway, as Charlie is otherwise engaged. She's going to a seventeenth birthday party at one of her friends' places. I told her to take the weekend off. I'll give Katy a call now, before she leaves work for the evening."

"You do that and I'll start on dinner. How does spag bol sound?"

Lorne kissed her husband on the cheek as she passed him on the way into the lounge. "Sounds like a wonderful idea to me." She heard pots and pans banging behind her, and thought back to the time when she had taught Tony to cook. She smiled at how far he'd come since the day he had forgotten to put water in with the pasta and she'd had to throw one of her best copper bottom pans away. He wouldn't dream of doing such a daft thing nowadays, after her superb guidance in the kitchen.

She picked up the phone and dialled Katy's mobile. A harassed Katy answered after the fifth ring, just before the voicemail kicked in. "Yesssss!" she hissed.

"Ah, I know that tone well. Is it a bad time? I can call back later, no problem."

"Nope, now's as good a time as any. Sorry, Lorne. My inept colleagues are just winding me up, that's all. How are things?"

Lorne could tell by Katy's tone that she didn't want to share what was bugging her, so Lorne avoided asking the obvious question. "What are you up to this weekend?"

Katy was silent for a while as she contemplated her answer. "Not much, why?"

"You're spending it with us. No arguments. I'm not having you spending your birthday alone. It'll just be the four of us."

"Four of us?" Katy asked, her voice softening.

"Yeah, the brat won't be here." Lorne chuckled. "You can have her room for the weekend."

"That'd be cool. I wasn't relishing the thought of being alone this weekend—not that I'm heavily into celebrating birthdays or anything. How's the centre doing?"

"Busy today. Listen, I don't want to hold you up any more than is necessary. However, I do need to ask a favour while I'm on the phone."

Katy lowered her voice and Lorne could hear the sound of Katy's shoes walking on the tiled corridor. "Shoot, I'm out of earshot of the team now."

Lorne chuckled, "Yeah, I can hear that it's still nice and echoey in the ladies' loo. I wondered if you knew anything about the boat that capsized in the storm off the Kent coast?"

"Dreadful story. Not heard anything as yet, only what I've seen on TV. Why?"

"Well you know what suspicious minds Tony, Dad, and I have. We thought it sounded like a human trafficking case."

"Hmm...I've been up to my eyes in it around here and not given it much thought, but looking at it objectively, you could be on to something. Why the interest? I mean, why this particular boat? There are hundreds of incidents like this that happen throughout the year. We're easy access for this kind of thing, what with the UK being an island, although it is a worldwide problem. Why has this one grabbed your attention, Lorne?"

"To begin with, I wasn't really sure. While I was watching the news, something in me began to stir. You know what happens when you get a gut feeling?"

"Yeah, I do. You said 'to begin with'—has something else happened?"

Lorne gave Katy a brief summary of what had happened at Natasha's house, and Katy listened without interruption.

"I see. Well, I can certainly see what I can dig up this end. Can I get back to you tomorrow? In fact, if you don't mind, I'll leave it 'til early afternoon; maybe I'll have more details to work with by then. What do you think?"

"Great idea. I'll wait for your call. Are you going to do this with or without Roberts's knowledge?"

"Without, for the time being. But if I stumble across anything worthwhile, I'll have to let him know. You know how it is."

"I understand, Katy. Speak to you tomorrow, then. Oh, and by the way, back to the weekend: is there anything you don't eat?"

"I can't stand that porridge stuff for breakfast. There's a reason they give it to the prisoners serving time."

Lorne laughed. "And that reason is?"

"Extra punishment, of course."

She had to laugh at the way Katy spat out the words. There was nothing wrong with porridge in Lorne's book. A good healthy breakfast set one up for the day. "I'll make sure we have all the ingredients for an unhealthy fry-up for your stay, then."

"Sounds fantastic. I'll get back to you after lunch tomorrow," Katy reminded her before they hung up.

Lorne joined the others in the kitchen. Tony turned to look at her when she walked into the room. He had tears streaming down his face. She walked over to him and dabbed at his cheeks with a tissue. "There, there, dear, no need to cry."

"Damn onions, they always seem to get their revenge."

"Forget the tip I gave you about putting a metal teaspoon in your mouth while you peel and cut them, did you? And you." She turned to her father and wagged her finger at him. "Why didn't you remind him how to combat the tears?"

Her father gave an innocent shrug. "What would be the fun in that? I like seeing another man cry, even if it is only over an onion!"

"Oh dear, and I thought *I* was the one with the mean streak."

"If you two have quite finished laughing at my expense. How did things go with Katy?"

"She sounded totally harassed, poor love. She's going to leave it 'til the morning, then start digging around for me."

"Makes sense to leave it another twelve hours or so," Tony said, placing the diced onions into a pan.

"Here, let me. It's taken you over ten minutes to slice one onion; I could've had the whole dinner knocked up in that time."

Her cheekiness earned her a whack on the backside with a tea towel.

CHAPTER FOUR

Derek Croft was sitting at his desk pounding a frantic rhythm on his computer keyboard, aware of the deadline creeping up on him. If he didn't get this story right, he'd have his notice in his hands by the end of the week. He looked up at the clock for the fifth time in as many minutes, then glanced at the silent phone sitting alongside his computer. *Ring, damn you, ring!* All he needed was a few snippets of information to complete his story, but his contact had let him down—again. Bloody informants were useless nowadays. Unreliable druggies, most of them, who took his money—*his* money, not the firm's—and ran to the nearest dealer to buy more drugs. The trouble was that these people knew what happened on the streets. Which was why these morons were vital to him.

His thoughts focused on the black phone, willing it to ring, but to no avail. After several more minutes of anxious staring that turned into teeth grinding accompanied by a glare, Croft decided that the only way his boss was going to be happy with his latest story was if he fabricated something a little juicy.

He closed his eyes and an image popped into his mind. He took it as an act of fate and ran with it, bugger the consequences.

The ill-fated vessel Spiritus *smashed against the rocks off the Kent coastline. So far, the captain and crew, numbers yet to be confirmed, have not been found. Twenty-five dead bodies have already been recovered by the coastguard. Most were found either on the rocks or floating in the bay. All the bodies that have been recovered in the wake of this terrible disaster have been of Asian origin and female. Sources have commented that these poor, unfortunate beings were doomed to a life of slavery and debauchery. Yes, folks, the slave trade is alive and growing on our wonderful shores.*

With drugs being seized at a phenomenal rate by undercover police in the capital, it means that the underworld gangs have been forced to turn to new pastures to sustain their lavish lifestyle. The trending crime appears to be that of human trafficking. Young Asian girls are being shipped, literally by the boatload, into London, where they are either sent to work in brothels or employed by some of Britain's wealthiest families.

More on this breaking story as we uncover further evidence.

Croft hit the save button, attached a copy of the file to an email, and sent it to his boss with thirty seconds to spare on his deadline. He relaxed back in his chair and expelled a heavy breath. *I hope I haven't overstepped the mark with this one.* As if on cue, one minute too late, his phone rang. "Croft speaking." He listened as his informant delivered the goods and smiled when he realised that what he had suspected about the incident had proved to be true. "Good work. You hear anything else, any names or places, ring me straight away, you got that?"

His informant answered him by hanging up, as he usually did. Seconds later, his boss bellowed out his name. Croft shot out of the chair as if it had just spontaneously combusted and sprinted to his boss's office.

He stood in the doorway, trembling from head to foot. "Yes, sir?"

"What the fuck do you call this, boy?" Trevor Moon waved the sheet of paper in front of him and screwed up his eyes.

Croft gripped the doorframe with his right hand for support. "I'm not sure what you mean, sir."

"Bullshit. That warning I gave you wasn't strong enough, I take it?" Moon threw the sheet of paper across the room in Croft's direction.

Croft hesitated, wondering if he should retrieve it or not. "Was the piece too short?"

"Too short, too sketchy, and too damn provocative. Based on lies or your imagination, I shouldn't wonder. What proof do you have?" Moon demanded.

Croft pulled his shoulders back, assured in his source, despite the information arriving *after* he'd sent his boss the copy. "Come on, boss. You know how these things go. You print that, and within minutes I bet your phone will be ringing off the hook. Bent coppers, councillors, and the like will all be demanding where you got your information. This story has legs." Croft cleared his throat, feeling confident that his boss looked more interested in his story now that he had challenged him. "If you don't want to run the story, I know plenty of papers who'd snap my hand off for a story like that."

"Bollocks! Like I said, there's no substance to the story. If you've made this up just to keep your job, you're a bigger fool than I've given you credit for over the last few months."

Croft shrugged. "Only one way to find out."

"Meaning?" Moon sneered.

"Let me do some digging. I'm an investigative journalist, after all, so let me investigate the story properly." Moon looked thoughtful, as if he were contemplating Croft's idea. Croft pushed his luck a little further. "How long has it been since this paper had a massive story, anyway? This could be the biggie we've been waiting for. Let me run with it. Print what I sent you. See it as a teaser to spark the public's curiosity, if you like."

"Last chance saloon for you, Croft. Fuck this up, and you'll be out of here as quick as that." He snapped his fingers to emphasise his threat.

Croft let out the breath he'd been holding and nodded. "Yes, boss."

"Now get out of here and go find me a story worth publishing."

Croft left the office and triumphantly punched the air. He'd just talked himself into at least another month's salary. Now all he had to do was find Moon his story. He picked up his rucksack, shoved his pen and notebook in it, and left the office with renewed vigour in his step.

CHAPTER FIVE

The following afternoon, Lorne received the call she had been waiting for. "Hi Katy, what did you find out?"

"Disappointing results so far. Maybe it's too soon after the incident for information to start filtering through. Here's what I do know: the search is still going on for the captain and the other crewmembers. They managed to find some of the hold still intact, and discovered another three bodies inside. Heartbreaking, the coastguard said—the girls were only about sixteen. They were found clinging to each other. I'm stating the obvious here, but they must have been scared shitless."

Lorne shook her head and sighed. "What a dreadful way to die. Crap, I really want to get the bastards who put these girls through this shit. Where do we start, though?"

"That's what I was wondering. The case won't really get underway until the rescuers have located all the bodies."

"I know. But Katy, how will we know how many people were stowed away? There's hardly going to be any records of the voyage, with cargo manifests, etc., is there?"

"These things have a habit of coming to light eventually. Let me do some more digging, and I'll get back to you if anything turns up."

Lorne ended the call, but before she could replace the portable phone in the docking station, it rang again. She recognised the number on the display and smiled as she answered it. "Hey, Sis, how's it going?"

"Give me strength. Hold on a sec, Lorne."

She could hear the beat of a child's drum set in the background, and then a child's scream when the noise ceased. "Why the hell did we buy him that?"

Laughing, Lorne replied, "I'm so glad you and Luigi bought the kids that drum set and not us. I would have hated getting the blame for them deafening you. Sounds like you have the next Phil Collins on your hands there."

"You think? Maybe we should nurture such raw talent, eh?"

Lorne chuckled at her sister's strained wit. "What can I do for you, Jade?"

Jade hesitated for a brief moment before she answered, "I'm not sure, really. It's probably nothing, but I thought I'd run it by you, just the same."

"You've piqued my interest now."

"You remember Angela North, don't you?"

After a brief pause, Lorne replied, "Umm…the girl you went to school with, you mean? Vaguely, why?"

"That's the one. Well, last year she got married out in the Maldives to a very wealthy guy."

Lorne whistled. "Nice to hear at least some people manage to land on their feet."

"Idiot. You'd be lost without Tony, and since when has money ever mattered to you?"

"Yeah, you have a point. So what's the problem—with Angela, I mean?"

"Well, she rang me in tears yesterday. Roger, her husband, employed an au pair to take care of Angela's stepson. This is Roger's second marriage; his first wife died about two years ago. He wouldn't tell her how his wife, Celia, died."

"I see, and…?"

"At first she found it hard to accept the au pair—jealousy, I'm guessing. But over the past few months, she's grown to really like and appreciate Jai San."

Lorne started making a wind up motion with her free hand. This was typical of Jade. She loved to gossip and stretch a story to its maximum, something that annoyed Lorne more often than not. "I hate to hurry you up, hon, but I have a few chores still left over from this morning that I have to complete before sunset."

"You cheeky cow! I'm getting there as fast as I can. Anyway, as I was saying before you so rudely interrupted me, the girl collapsed last night, for no reason. When she woke up it took Angela over three hours to worm the problem out of her. And Lorne, it's horrendous. I'm shaking just thinking about what that girl must be going through."

"Jade! *Please* get to the point."

"You always were the most impatient person I've ever had the privilege of knowing," Jade said, her frustration evident.

"Yeah, and you've always been the most melodramatic person I know, but that doesn't mean I love you any less. Tell me, for goodness sake!"

"I'm not sure if you saw what happened in the storm?"

"Yeah, it was all over the news. I know the roads were terrible to get by. Was the house hit by a tree or something? Was someone badly injured?"

"Listen, will you?" Jade snapped back in annoyance. "It's been in the news, every hour on the hour—you must have seen it. That ship, boat, whatever you call it, that was ripped apart in the storm."

Lorne gasped. She had an inkling she knew what was coming next. She'd momentarily drifted off, and the sound of her sister's voice shouting through the phone brought her out of her reverie.

"Lorne? Are you listening to me?"

"Sorry, Jade. What about the ship?"

"I just bloody told you. Jai San's sister was aboard. She's dead. She was sixteen, for Christ's sake. *Sixteen!*" said Jade, overreacting as she always did when she knew someone involved in something traumatic.

"Damn," Lorne muttered under her breath.

"Damn! Damn, is that all you can say? I expected more from you. I thought you'd be interested after what they're saying about this boat."

"Sorry, Jade, my mind is elsewhere. Obviously it's a sickening situation, truly awful. Can you make arrangements for me to visit your friend perhaps?"

"Of course, I'll give Angela a call," Jade said, her tone softening a little, "and get back to you later."

Lorne spent the rest of the afternoon distracted and deep in thought. *What were the odds of two of the victims having family employed by people she knew? How rife had human trafficking become?* After the case with the Unicorn, Lorne had hoped that certain restrictions had been put in place to help combat the heinous crime, but obviously it wasn't enough. She felt sickened that people were still being abused in this manner. If only she had a government contact who could give her an inside take on what they were doing to combat this abhorrent crime in this so called civilised part of the world.

"What's wrong, love?" Tony came up behind her chair and massaged her shoulders.

Of course, Tony. She tilted her head to the side and rested her cheek on the back of one of his hands. "The usual—busy thinking."

He squeezed her shoulder and then sat in the chair next to her. "About the shipwreck?"

She nodded, and thought for a second or two before she spoke again, "How friendly are you with MI6/5 at the moment?"

Tony's eyes rose to the ceiling and he inhaled deeply. "I know where you're going with this, and I'm not sure I want to go down that road, hon."

"Not even when innocent people are being brutalised and victimised in this way? You'd be *happy* to sit back and watch that happen, would you? Don't forget what happened to you in Afghanistan!" She paused. "Sorry, hon, that was a bit harsh."

Tony fell back in his chair. "That's not fair and you know it. The authorities have this case in hand. Let's see what happens in the next day or two, huh?"

"They could take weeks to sift through the wreckage. The victims' families need some form of justice now."

"Lorne, you know how these things work—"

She cut him off with a raised hand and an angry look. "Please don't give me that tired old cliché about Rome not being built in a day."

"Okay, I won't. But you know it's true."

"Yeah, I know you're right. That doesn't mean to say that it's any less frustrating. I want to get on and try to do something to help these poor people get out of the situation they're in. It's too late for some of them, but there are probably thousands more out there caught up in similar positions. I can't help thinking that the ones killed in that horrific storm are better off dead, compared to the sickening alternative. It's the thousands of people out there being shunted around from country to country to the highest bidder who I want—*need*—to help. I know what my daughter went through. That poor girl—Sasha—who tried to help Charlie was forced to endure the dreadful sight of her own family being burned at the stake, and her captors did it just to keep her in line. These innocent people are treated worse than animals by scum wanting to line their pockets."

All the way through her ranting speech, Tony's eyes remained fixed firmly on hers. She knew he felt the same way as she did, and she admired the way he could keep a lid on his anger—something she lacked.

"The slave trade has been with us since the year dot, Lorne. I doubt that will ever change. You may be Wonder Woman in most regards, but I don't think even you'll be able to do much to alter things in that respect."

"You're probably right, as usual, but I'm not prepared to give up now, Tony."

"I never doubted that for a second."

CHAPTER SIX

Derek Croft left his office faster than a Formula One racecar once the call came in. He had a fire in his belly that was causing havoc with his newly diagnosed ulcer. He'd spent most of the day on the phone to several of his informants, mostly with negative results, until half an hour ago, when Sammy had called him. The twenty-year-old druggie had never let him down in the past, so Croft knew it was imperative to get over to the site ASAP. Or as fast as his battered old VW Golf would carry him.

With night already setting in, he screeched to a halt and parked several roads from the location he'd been given. The area was a built-up industrial zone, quiet after a busy day's trading. An icy chill flowed through his veins that had nothing to do with the air temperature when he got out of the car. Armed with his camera, he ran down one narrow road and then the next, until he found the address Sammy had suggested where he would find what he was after. Several stray dogs roamed the vicinity looking for scraps, but they scattered in different directions when he dashed past them.

Croft scanned the area for a possible hideaway observation point. He was in the process of settling himself behind a massive industrial metal dumpster when he heard a distant vehicle approaching. He threw himself behind his chosen cover and peeked out to watch a large ten-tonne truck pull to a halt in front of the gates, obscuring his view. He mentally kicked himself for not being able to take any pictures; if he used his camera in the fading light, the flash would kick in, automatically giving away his whereabouts.

Once the metal railing gates had been opened, the truck drove through the opening and stopped on the other side. A large bruiser of a guy jumped down from the cab. After high-fiving the two men already waiting in the yard, the driver stretched out the muscles in his back before the three of them shared a joke and moved to the rear of the truck.

Croft inched forward and craned his neck, but his view was limited. Now he had a dilemma: did he move position and risk getting caught, or did he sit tight in the hope that he'd hear and eventually see something useful? Once the men had moved to the back of the truck, his limited view became even more restricted. He couldn't decipher the murmuring voices. His frustration mounted and grew tenfold within seconds, forcing him to rethink his strategy.

Taking advantage of the noise the men were making as they unlatched the doors to the truck, Croft snuck out from behind the dumpster and crept several feet closer, but he couldn't find anything else suitable to hide behind. Defeated, and conscious that he might blow his cover, Croft returned to his original position.

He heard the men shouting orders, then numerous slaps, followed by screams and men's laughter. *Shit! Sammy was spot on. There are girls on that truck.* Panicked by the knowledge, Croft's heart pounded harder against his ribcage. *What the fuck have I stumbled across here? Are the girls kept here? Moved elsewhere? What a story!* However, without photographic evidence, he knew he'd have a hard time selling it to his boss." *I should call the authorities. Fuck that! I need this job. I need this story!*

It was another twenty minutes before the yard fell quiet. He didn't have a clue how many people had been transferred inside the building. He settled back on his haunches, pulled his jacket up around his neck to ward off the draft, and prepared to wait it out for the next few hours. *I bet the bastards are in there groping the girls.*

Several hours later, Croft was startled awake by activity as the truck started up and the gates were flung open. He held his breath as the truck stopped outside the gates and two men jumped into the cab. With the driver already behind the wheel, he assumed that the three men he'd seen inside the yard had all just vacated the area in the truck. He decided to give it another five minutes before he made his move.

Cautiously, he approached the gates. They were high, but not insurmountable. The only problem he could foresee was if there were any hidden cameras angled at the gates recording his movements. Did he have the bottle to attempt to climb them? *Nope! I don't.*

He decided to go home and write up the story. A story that his boss was either going to praise him or sack him for in the morning when he placed it on his desk.

CHAPTER SEVEN

Lorne read the article in the national newspaper, her mouth dropping open in horror. She'd had dealings with this particular journalist over the years and hadn't liked him one bit, but something about the way he'd had the balls to write the story others had so far avoided made her admire his courage.

"What's that, love?" Tony asked as he came down for breakfast. After flicking the switch on the kettle, he sat down beside her at the table.

Lorne handed him the paper without saying a word.

Tony was quiet for several minutes, absorbed in the story, until he let out an ear-splitting whistle. "He's either very brave, or bloody stupid."

"For running the story?"

Tony glanced up at her. "Er…yeah. Do you know this reporter guy?"

"I've had certain dealings with him in the past. Pete used to call him 'the Ferret.' He never liked to leave a stone unturned on a story. The dirtier the details, the better, as far as he was concerned. He used to hound me for days trying to be the first to get the scoop on some of the nastier cases I had to deal with at the Met." Tony's expression turned thoughtful, prompting Lorne to ask, "What's going on in that head of yours?"

"Think about it. The other day, you were asking me about my contacts in MI6. Now it looks to me like this guy has his finger firmly on the pulse of this story."

"I couldn't get in touch with *him*."

Tony shrugged. "Not sure you have any other options left open to you. So far, Katy hasn't come up with much to go on. It's all been hush-hush from her end, which to me stinks of something."

Lorne frowned. "A cover-up?"

"Maybe. Look at all the high profile people who were connected with Charlie's case. All those dignitaries intent on getting their end away with those unfortunate teenage girls. What happened to the filthy bastards? Nothing, absolutely fuck all. Even though we had CCTV evidence to prove they attended that 'auction of human flesh,' the bastards got away with it, as usual."

Heat erupted through her veins at the thought of dirty old men getting away with treating young girls in such a deplorable way. It seemed the more corrupt you were, the easier life became. Perhaps Tony had a point about using Croft. He obviously had good contacts at his disposal to get the inside take on this story.

Tony interrupted her thoughts to add, "Go on, swallow your pride and give him a call. Between us, I think we could make a difference. If we all tackled this case as individuals, we could get in each other's way and these guys could get away with it for years to come. Let's try and put *this* gang out of action, at least. What do you say?"

Lorne's indecision didn't hang around for long. "Okay, you win!" She left the kitchen and walked into the lounge, she picked up the phone and dialled the number on the card she had retrieved from her handbag. "Derek?" It shocked her to hear him answer after only one ring.

"Yep, who's this?"

"Umm...Lorne Warner...er...I guess you'd remember me as Simpkins, though."

"Well what do you know? The great Simpkins ringing me for a change, who'd have thunk it?"

His attitude hadn't changed one iota since she'd last dealt with him. He always came across as cocksure and arrogant. She kept calm in spite of wanting to hang up and end the conversation before it had begun. The guy was a creep, but she needed him, as he seemed to be the only one with any answers. "I was wondering if we could meet up for a chat?"

He laughed. "A chat, you say. I wonder what that could be about—the price of groceries skyrocketing since the recession started? Nah, not your style, Simpkins, is it?"

"Cut the crap, Croft. You know what about. I'm not going to beg. Yes or no?"

Amusement filling his voice, he said, "Ahh, you're interested in the case I've blown wide open, I take it."

Lorne clenched her free hand a few times before she responded. "I just think we could be of service to each other, if you're willing to give it a shot." There was silence on the other end of the line, something that Lorne hadn't expected. "Are you still there, Croft?"

"I'm here. Name the time and place and I'll be there. I'm pretty flexible, as you know; during work hours or after it makes no odds to me."

Lorne quickly ran through in her mind what she had planned for the rest of the day, and decided the best option would be to meet in town somewhere after work. "What about this evening, about seven-ish?"

"Suits me. Where?"

"I'm kind of out of touch; your choice."

"Okay, the wine bar on Kilburn High Street—how does that sound?" Croft said.

Like a very long trip for me, but what the heck. "Sounds great. See you then."

"Look forward to it, Lorne." His smarmy tone and the way he said her name left her feeling cold. Little did the Ferret know that Tony would be at the meeting, as well. She couldn't wait to see the look on Croft's face when she turned up with her husband in tow.

Lorne hung up and shuddered as she stepped back into the kitchen. "Eww...he's such a creep. I have a feeling we're going to live to regret this."

Tony sniggered. "What did he say?"

"I didn't go into detail; I just asked him to meet me. I didn't mention you'd be there, of course. Shit, you are going to be there, aren't you? I don't think I could handle meeting him by myself."

"Don't fret, I'll be there. When and where are we meeting up?"

Lorne blew out the breath she had been holding. "Seven o'clock tonight, in Kilburn."

Her father came into the kitchen. "What's that, love?"

Lorne hesitated before mentioning the rendezvous, unsure of what her father's reaction would be. "Tony and I have a meeting in town this evening, Dad."

"What type of meeting?"

Lorne glanced over at her husband for help, but received none. "We're having a drink with a journalist about the possible trafficking case down in Kent."

"Why?" her father asked, looking puzzled.

Lorne sat down heavily in the nearest chair. "Because we need to act on this quickly, while these guys are still in the area."

"Fair enough." Her father's words surprised her. Then he changed the subject, which surprised her even more. "What's for dinner tonight? If you two are going out, I can fix myself something, it's no bother."

"I'll get out a couple of lamb chops for you and peel some veg before we go, if that's all right."

Her father gave a slight nod and seemed happy with her choice. He turned around and left the kitchen, heading back to his bedroom.

"Well, that was weird," she said after hearing his door close. "I expected him to kick up a fuss. He hates journalists more than I hate black pudding."

"Maybe he has other things on his mind."

Hmm…like what?

CHAPTER EIGHT

The drive into London went easier than expected; Lorne surmised that maybe partygoers stayed away from the City during the week and let rip only at the weekend. However, when they finally located the wine bar where Lorne had arranged to meet Croft, it was bustling with activity. Lorne scanned the dozens of full tables, and after a few seconds made eye contact with Croft. The Ferret had burrowed himself into a dark corner at the back of the bar—was that on purpose? As they approached his table, Lorne watched the smile on his face slip and give way to a scowl when he saw Tony walking behind her.

"Derek."

"Lorne. Who's this? I thought we'd be meeting alone," Croft said, shifting uncomfortably in his seat.

"Sorry, did I forget to mention that I'd be bringing along my partner? Tony Warner, meet journalist Derek Croft."

Neither of the men held out a hand to shake the other's, and Croft eyed Tony with caution. The Ferret felt trapped. Lorne pushed down a snigger that was threatening to escape.

"Partner in what, exactly? I heard you left the Met a couple of years ago."

"Ah, in a few things, actually. In life as well as two businesses, one of which is a private investigation firm."

Croft cracked a smile. "For real? Like Magnum P.I. type of thing?"

Lorne shrugged. "If you like. Right, enough of the small talk. Let's get down to it, shall we?"

"Yeah, I'm dying to know why you rang me. Although, things are starting to lock into place now."

"I read your article on the human trafficking incident you witnessed the other day. How did you get away with writing a story like that, Derek?"

"My contact on the street told me it was going down, so I ran it past my boss and he told me to get on it."

Tony asked, "You do know the type of people you're dealing with here, don't you?"

Croft looked at Tony as if he'd just escaped from an asylum. He pointed his thumb in Tony's direction and asked Lorne, "Is he for real?"

Lorne's hand instinctively sought out Tony's wrist to prevent him giving Croft a bop on the nose. "It was a serious question, Derek. Do you know who you're dealing with?"

"Yeah. Scum! Scum of the earth. That's why I intend bringing the fuckers down."

"That's commendable of you, but also more than a tad foolish," Lorne said, smiling at him.

"Yeah I know, but needs must. Why are you so interested in the case anyway?"

"I'm not. No, that's a lie. I'm interested in finding out a little more about what you know, but basically I'm more interested in a different case. I have an inkling that the two cases are probably connected."

"Not sure I'm following you," Croft said.

"The ship that capsized at the beginning of the week—my instincts tell me that we're looking at a human trafficking operation. It's yet to be confirmed, of course, but—"

"But you have firsthand experience in such cases, and your antenna is urging you to get involved," he finished the sentence for her.

Lorne laughed. "You know, Derek, for a hard-nosed journo writing a load of bullshit most of the time, you can be quite perceptive when you want to be."

"Yeah, I have many different faces. I'm kinda like you in that respect."

Lorne knew he wasn't insulting her and that his assumption was accurate enough; at least it used to be, when she was on the force. Not so much nowadays, but if the need arose, then she could and would easily revert back to her old ways. "You're probably right. What do you say, then? Are you willing to pool our information to crack the case?"

He drifted off for a second or two as he thought over her plan. "It depends."

"On what, exactly?" Lorne asked. He smirked, and an unwelcome shiver ran up her spine. Despite his boyish good looks, there was something intensely creepy about Croft. However, she'd already decided that she would be willing to put aside her uneasiness in order to get the information she needed.

"On what information you've got. So far, I think my contacts have come up with a lot, but like I said, it depends what you can throw into the pot."

"I'm waiting on a couple of calls. I'm not willing to divulge what I have so far—" She stopped talking and her mouth dropped open when Croft thrust out of his chair and headed for the door. *What the fuck was that all about?*

Tony was the first out of his chair, with Lorne close behind him. They caught up with the Ferret, who had set off like a greyhound in the car park outside. Croft made it to his car and had inserted the key in the driver's door before they caught up with him. Annoyed that the journalist had walked out on them mid-conversation, Tony pinned Croft against the side of his car, and Lorne did nothing to stop her husband.

"Get your filthy hands off me," Croft said, more out of shock than anger.

"Didn't your mother ever tell you that it's rude to walk out when someone is talking to you?" Tony asked with a raised eyebrow and his forearm tight across Croft's throat.

"Fuck off. We're here to swap information, so far that ain't happening, is it?" Croft managed to say through a restricted windpipe.

Tony jabbed him in the stomach with a clenched fist. Croft coughed and spluttered, glancing at Lorne for help. She folded her arms and stared back at him. "Did I forget to mention that Tony is ex-MI6? Silly me. Shall we try and start this meeting again in a calm and friendly manner? What do you say, Croft?"

"Call the gorilla off, and I'll think about it."

Lorne noticed a tremble had developed in Croft's voice. She nodded for Tony to let go of him. Croft straightened his jacket and rubbed his throat with his hand.

"Why don't we sit in your car and finish our conversation?"

Croft glared at Tony as he spoke. "On one condition. He sits up front with me where I can keep an eye on him."

"I can do that," Tony replied with a grin.

Croft pressed the button on his key fob and the car unlocked with a *clunk*. The three of them got in, the two men in the front and Lorne behind the passenger seat so Croft could talk directly to her without wondering what she was up to behind his back.

Lorne started the conversation off. "If you had let me finish, I was going to say that I'm not willing to divulge what I have at the moment because things are a little sketchy and I wouldn't want to muddy the water."

"Ah, then that's different. Sorry for any misunderstanding."

Lorne smiled at Croft, appreciating his apology. "Have you had any feedback from anyone about the story you ran?"

Croft laughed. "By 'feedback,' I take it you mean threatening calls. Yeah, I've had a couple of those. Which only goes to prove that I'm on to something big."

"I'd say you've more than rattled a few cages. Can I ask why you ran the story? Naming names the way you did?"

"To be honest, I was in a no-win situation—either I ran the story, or my boss was going to fire me."

Tony whistled. "Nice boss. So now your life is permanently in danger."

Croft's nose screwed up. "I wouldn't say that. I can deal with these guys. I've dealt with scummier dirtbags than these over the years."

Lorne couldn't believe the naïvety of the man. "What kind of threats have they issued? I take it we're talking about over the phone?" Croft nodded, so Lorne continued, "Were the calls to your mobile or your landline?"

"Both," he said, and shrugged as though it didn't bother him.

"Have you noticed anyone following you?"

Croft shook his head. "You worry too much. I'll be fine. Once the police have rounded these dirtbags up and locked them away, things will be cool again."

"You really don't have a clue how these things work, do you? Mess with one guy, and he has a whole army of men under him. I doubt very much if you'll ever bring down the top man, because one of his soldiers will always put himself forward to take the rap—at a cost, of course. He and his family will be taken care of until the day he's released from prison. We're talking a multi-billion dollar business here, and as we all know, money talks."

"Nah, you're wrong. The names I've been given are small fry."

"You've not listened to a word my wife has said, have you?" Tony shook his head and sneered at the Ferret.

Croft thought about this for a few seconds before a light bulb appeared to spark to life in his brain. "So what you're saying is that we need to find out who the organ grinder is to the operation."

At last, the penny drops and you call yourself an investigative journalist. "What's happening next on your end?"

"I don't understand," Croft said, perplexed.

"Are you supposed to be running a follow-up story? Have you been back to the warehouse where you saw the girls being unloaded to see if there has been any more activity?" Lorne asked, letting out a heavy breath.

"Well, Moon—that's my boss—wants me to run another story at the end of next week. It's Thursday today, and he wants the next installment on his desk seven days from now, at the latest, ready for Friday's edition."

"Where do you get your information?" Lorne asked him.

He tapped his nose and winked at her. "Now that would be telling, wouldn't it? It's accurate, that's all you need to know."

Before either Lorne or Tony could question him further, the sound of screeching tyres filled the car. Lorne had just turned to look out of the back window when she felt the impact. Shouting broke out inside the vehicle as it was forced forward. The black tinted windows of the four-by-four blocked out the identity of their attacker. Everything appeared to happen in slow motion, until the front of Croft's car connected with the rear wall of the wine bar. The last thing Lorne heard was a sickening crunch.

Lorne had no idea how long she'd been unconscious, a man's scream jolted her awake. "What the...?"

The inside of the car was dimly lit by the streetlight to the left of them, and the first thing that caught her eye was the way the bonnet of the car had concertinaed and was now positioned halfway up the windscreen. She looked at Croft; he had blood running down his face from a wound on his forehead. He was less concerned about his own injuries, though, and was frantically pointing to the passenger seat. Scared, Lorne leaned forward and frantically shook her husband's shoulder. "Tony?"

He mumbled something under his breath as he came around, but she couldn't make out what it was. Then she broke the silence in the car by laughing like a demented dog. It wasn't long before Tony realised what she was laughing at and joined in.

"You two are sick. What the fuck's wrong with you? Look!"

Tony reached down beside him and pulled up the thing that had shocked Croft so much. The guy looked as though he were going to vomit any second as Tony waved his leg in the air.

Lorne heard Croft gag. She placed a comforting hand on his shoulder. "It's all right—it's a false leg."

Croft let out a relieved breath and held his head in his hands. "Jesus Christ. I had no idea. To see the bloody thing lying there like that…"

Tony laughed. "Guess I better take a trip to the hospital to see what damage has been done." He ran his hands down either side of the prosthetic limb and winced. "Won't be able to use this one again, the state it's in."

"Any other injuries, either of you?" Lorne asked.

Croft checked himself over and looked down at the blood on his hands that had come from a wound on his forehead. "It's just a scratch, I think." Lorne watched him wiggle his legs beneath the steering wheel, which had surprisingly remained intact.

"I'm good. How are you, hon?" Tony asked, smiling at her.

"I'm good… Well, I suppose we'd better make the call to report this little incident. Did either of you see anything?" Both men shook their heads. "The windows were blacked out. I noticed the plates were removed. I'll bet that car intentionally hit us; this is more than a hit-and-run by a scared teenager."

"Yep, that seems suspicious in itself. Oops, we seem to be attracting an audience." Tony said, pointing at the gathering crowd.

Lorne eased open the back door and stepped out onto the tarmac of the car park. Under the gaze of the crowd, none of whom rushed to offer any form of help, she fished her mobile out of her jacket pocket and dialled 9-9-9.

"Yes, police, please. There's been an accident. No, no one was injured. Only the police need to attend." She gave the girl on the switchboard the location and hung up.

Tony got out of the vehicle and flung an arm around Lorne's shoulders for support.

"I'll deal with the police when they arrive. I'll tell them we were chatting with an acquaintance in his car, and then some guy hit us from behind with his car and drove off. I'll settle you in our car before they arrive." Lorne helped Tony over to her father's Nova, which was thankfully parked on the other side of the car park out of harm's way, near the entrance. After settling Tony in the front seat, she returned to Croft's beat-up vehicle and surveyed the damage.

"Hey, it's a good job I've been considering a replacement," Croft said, standing alongside her.

In spite of what had happened, Lorne was amazed at how matter of fact he was being. Despite someone trying their hardest to frighten the hell out of them, he appeared totally chilled out; others might have been shaking in their boots by now.

Lorne shook her head. "Now do you see who you're dealing with?"

Croft shrugged nonchalantly. "Makes no odds to me. I've got them on the run."

"You really don't get it at all. These guys mean business, Croft. This was a warning, that's all. If they had really wanted to harm you, they could've just killed us."

"Yeah, but I've got a magic weapon now. I've got the great DI Lorne Simpkins working with me."

His words forced a smile out of her, but left her wondering if she really had it in her these days to deal with the dirtiest criminals around. There was only one way to find out.

CHAPTER NINE

By the time they'd given a statement to the police and taken Tony to the hospital to get checked over, it was late, and it was past midnight when they got home.

Lorne was surprised to find her father still up and pacing around the kitchen waiting for them to come home. "Hi, Dad, everything all right?"

"I couldn't flaming sleep. You guys are late."

"Yeah, later than we anticipated." Not wishing to cause her father any unnecessary worry, Lorne hesitated before telling him what had occurred in the last few hours. But the expression on his face told her he had already guessed that some form of trouble had found them.

"Okay, what went on?"

Lorne, Tony, and her father slumped into the chairs around the table and Lorne proceeded to fill her father in. He listened intently, without interruption. After she had finished, he reached for her hand and squeezed it. "Christ! Are you sure you're okay? Must have been a hell of a fright."

"And then some. Yeah, we're both fine, Dad. The hospital gave Tony a temporary limb to use until a replacement can be made. They gave him the all-clear, too. I just hope Croft recovers from his ordeal of seeing Tony's leg lying there." She laughed to break the tension. "Any calls while we were out, Dad?"

"Actually, yes. Jade called. She said something about arranging a meeting with one of her friends."

"Angie—that's right."

"I said you'd give her a call first thing for a chat."

"That's brilliant. Let's hope I can meet up with her soon. The sooner the better, if tonight's little tangle is anything to go by."

They all said goodnight and set off to bed. Lorne spent the night snuggled into Tony's back, scared to let him go.

* * *

Lorne groaned and hit the alarm beside her bed. Sometimes she hated getting up before the sun rose. Henry licked her face. "All right, I'm coming."

She trudged downstairs and let the dog out the back door before she filled the kettle and then flicked the switch. The morning felt crisp, and the mist she could see in the dim light hinted that the day ahead would be a pleasant one.

After letting the dog back in and feeling more awake, she ran upstairs and threw on her work clothes. An hour later, she had finished all the basic chores outside in the kennels and headed back inside the house. Her father was sitting at the table, waiting for her.

"Good morning." She pecked him on the forehead and gazed down at him. His skin looked pale, but she knew better than to point it out. "Did you sleep well?"

"Not really. I was too busy worrying about you."

"Aww...come on, Dad. There's no need for that, I'm a big girl now," she teased, flinging her arms around his neck and planting another kiss on the top of his head.

"No matter what age you are, you're still my baby. Promise me you'll be careful on this case, Lorne."

"Hey, that goes without saying, Dad. I'm always careful. Don't forget I've got Tony by my side, too. That means we have twice the muscle and the brainpower. It's Croft we've got to be wary of. He's like a bull in a china shop, that one."

"If anything, he's my main concern in all this. No point in having a word with him, I suppose," her father said.

She exhaled a large breath. "Believe me, I've tried. Even after last night's incident, I tried to tell him that these guys mean business, told him he should take what happened as a serious warning, but I can't see him doing that."

"Then why work with him? Why put yourself in jeopardy like that, love?"

"Hey, come on, Dad, this isn't like you. You've always given me credit in the common sense department. What's with the doubts this time?"

"A gut feeling I have. I'll back off under the proviso that you'll be extra vigilant on this case. You know how tetchy these criminals get if their income is interfered with."

"I'll be careful—that goes without saying. Anyway old man, Tony won't let anything happen to me." Lorne could tell by the look on her father's face that he remained unconvinced by her words. "I know he was with me last night, but we didn't see the car before it struck us."

"Right..." was all her father said before he left the room.

That went well! She watched him walk up the passage, but he stopped midway and hit the palm of his hand on his forehead, then walked back towards her.

"Sorry, mind like a sieve. I wanted to remind you to ring Jade first thing."

"I will, Dad." She took a few steps forward and kissed his cheek. "And don't worry about me, promise?"

He smiled at her, but the smile never reached his eyes. He turned away without uttering another word.

Knowing how hectic Jade's morning was with two toddlers in the house, Lorne left it until nine o'clock before she rang her sister.

"Hi, Jade, how's the tribe?"

"Remind me again why I wanted a handful of kids? I'm so glad I decided to stop at two."

Lorne laughed. "Hey, that's one more than I managed to cope with. Driving you to distraction, are they?"

"Yeah, you could say that. I need a kind and caring auntie to volunteer to take them off my hands for a few days while hubby and I have a break."

"Ah, well, ordinarily I would jump at the chance—you know that—but if you and Luigi went away together, you'd probably come back pregnant again. Think of your two being a cheap version of contraception."

"You're just too practical for words sometimes, Sis."

"I aim to please. Dad said you called last night."

"Yeah, I finally tracked Angie down; you know she's the type to do lunches and charity balls, etc. She says that she can fit you in sometime this afternoon, around four-ish. Does that suit you?"

"Nice of her to squeeze me into her busy schedule. Will Jai San be there, too?"

"As far as I know, yeah. I'll ring her back and confirm it, then, shall I? If I don't call back, you'll know I've managed to fix the appointment for you. You have the address, don't you?"

"I have. Thanks, Jade. I hope the kids don't play you up too much today."

Lorne hung up just as Tony entered the kitchen. "Looks like I have an appointment this afternoon with Jade's friend."

"That's great. What time?" he replied, giving her a cuddle.

"Four. I'm going to chase up Katy this morning, too. I'm not happy that the police aren't making this case a priority, it's all too quiet for me."

"It does seem strange, especially after all the publicity."

"In fact, I think I'll ring her now. I'll sort your breakfast out in a moment, hon."

"Do what you have to do. I'm quite capable of throwing a few slices of bread in the toaster. I'll be sure to watch for the smoke coming out the top."

Lorne shook her head and tutted at her husband's joke. She picked up the phone and dialled Katy's number. "Hi, any news?"

"I was going to share all I had over the weekend, not that I've found out much. It's looking more like a cover-up the more I delve into things," Katy told her in a hushed voice. "Hold on a sec, I'll go through to the office. Yep, AJ, I need that info ASAP before I go out." There was a moment's pause before Katy spoke again. "Sorry about that. Can't talk for long, just on my way out to arrest someone. Look, the more I dig into things, the more the barriers are going up. I spend half my day trying to ring people to find out some kind of information about the ship that went down, but no one returns my calls. Roberts is getting a bit antsy about the time I'm spending on the case, too, so I have to be careful."

"I understand. Why do you think information is proving difficult to come by?"

"I'm guessing there are some pretty high up people involved in this. You know how these things go, Lorne. It galls me to think of these people getting away with this. Have you managed to find anything out?"

"As it happens, yes. I'm meeting up with one of Jade's friends later. The woman's au pair had a sister on board the ill-fated ship. Also, yesterday Tony and I met the journalist who ran the story. We met him and had a pretty eventful evening. I'll fill you in over the weekend. Are you still coming tomorrow?"

"That's a definite. I can't wait to be with sane people."

Lorne chuckled. "You'd better go elsewhere for the weekend if that's the case, then."

"Got to go. See you tomorrow."

* * *

Lorne jumped in the car at a quarter past three and was en route to Angie's house when it occurred to her that maybe she should have left the meeting with Angie until the weekend; it would have been better to have had Katy's perspective on things and to team up with her former partner again. Deep down, she missed the rapport she'd once had with Katy. Actually, this weekend it had been Lorne's intention to try and persuade Katy to join the firm; the only stumbling block Lorne could see was the question of salary. They'd never be able to afford to match her Met salary yet, not until the business really took off.

She turned in through the gates of the large mansion house, which was not dissimilar to the Wallaces's house she had visited a few days earlier. Archetypical for the wealthy—stinking rich brigade in the London area, Lorne guessed. She drove past an army of men tending the beautiful garden who appeared to be redesigning one of the beds, ripping out the spring bulbs and making way for the abundance of summer bedding plants that were lined up in trays in regimented lines along the drive. She suspected that if she stayed around long enough, she would be privy to military precision at its finest.

A butler rushed out of the house and opened the door to Lorne's car when she pulled up outside the front entrance. Embarrassed, she smiled at the wizened old man. "Sorry, have I parked in the wrong place?"

The butler seemed surprised by her question. "No, ma'am, I'm just opening the door for you. Mrs. North is expecting you. Walk this way, please." The butler shuffled up the hallway.

If I walk like that, mate, your mistress will think that I'm some kind of primate, she thought before reprimanding herself for being grossly unkind and insensitive to the man's obvious disability.

The hallway of the house took Lorne's breath away. A large, sweeping galleried staircase, which appeared to be very Americanised for the house, greeted her. If it had been any other house of this era, Lorne had the feeling the staircase would have looked out of place, but the way this one was designed with its backdrop of windows was truly spectacular.

The butler coughed slightly to gain her attention. "This way, ma'am."

"Sorry, interior design fascinates me and I've never seen anything quite so beautiful."

"Ah. Mrs. North employed the services of a top architect when she purchased the house five years ago. This area alone took almost six months to complete."

"I can believe it."

He showed her through a small hallway and into a vast lounge at the rear of the property. Angela North was sitting in a winged chair alongside the open bi-fold doors. The petite lady was smartly dressed in a cream-coloured pencil skirt and a chocolate boucle buttoned-up cardigan. She stood and limply shook hands with Lorne.

"You have a beautiful house, Mrs. North."

The comment brought a sparkle to the woman's eyes and a tinge of colour to her cheeks. When she spoke, her voice was gentle and barely above a whisper. "You're very kind. Not everyone appreciates the alterations I've made to the house."

"I'm surprised. You have an excellent eye for detail."

"Thank you, that means a lot. Would you care for a tea or coffee?"

"A coffee would be nice, thank you."

The butler left the room while Angela motioned for Lorne to sit on the white leather sofa opposite her chair. As they sat, Lorne's eye was immediately drawn to the landscaped gardens and the beautiful open countryside beyond.

After seeing the admiration on Lorne's face, Angela said, "Isn't it beautiful? I spend most of my day just taking in the view. I've always loved this house—more for the location than anything else. A house can be altered to your specifications, but you can't change a view—that's what my father always told me."

"He's right. If ever I win the lottery, I might come and make an offer on this place; it has to be my dream home. You'd probably send me off with a flea in my ear for being so cheeky."

Angela smiled proudly. "They're going to have to carry me out in a box, I think. Anyway, enough of my luxuries I know you're a very busy lady—let's get down to this awful tragedy." Sadness swept her smile away and tears moistened her eyes.

"Jade told me your au pair had a relative in the disaster—is she here?"

"Do you mind if I introduce you later? She's very timid. I thought I could fill in the details for you first, if you don't mind."

Lorne nodded reassuringly. "Of course I don't mind. It must be hard for Jai San to be in a strange country having to deal with something so tragic."

"It is. She's such a sweet girl. My heart really goes out to her."

"Has she worked for you long, Angela?"

"About six months, I suppose. She was so excited when she learned her sister would be joining her here. When I say 'here,' I mean in the UK, not here in this house. My little Anthony absolutely idolises her. Before she came into our lives, he used to drive me and his previous au pairs to distraction. Throwing temper tantrums every minute of the day—I don't mind telling you I was at my wit's end. She has a calmness that surrounds her. Does that sound strange?"

"An aura, you mean?"

"Not exactly. She's a Buddhist. I know I'd be lost without her. My days at the charity can be stressful enough, you see I'm a bit of a soft touch where Anthony's concerned and he tends to play on that when I get home. His tantrums getting more and more out of hand and were having a detrimental effect on my sanity until she came along."

Lorne understood completely where Angela was coming from—her own daughter Charlie hadn't been the easiest child to bring up. Not that Lorne had brought Charlie up, per se; that onerous task had been down to Tom, her ex, most of the time. During her teens, Charlie had been a devil child, and even before she had reached her teens, she had demanded Tom's attention throughout most of the day. Rather than get into the whys and wherefores of parenting with a stranger, knowing the subject could be as volatile as politics or religion to some people, therefore avoided at all cost, Lorne steered the conversation back to Jai San. "Can I ask how you found your au pair? Did she come recommended?"

Angela thought for a second or two before she responded. "Well, like I said, I had worked my way through numerous au pairs—or Anthony had. Let me think. Do you know, I can't for the life of me remember. How bloody silly of me."

"It really doesn't matter." Lorne stopped talking as the sound of a rattling tray filled the room and the butler approached them.

"Thank you, Harry." Angela smiled at the bent old man and patted his hand affectionately when he placed the tray down on the table beside her. "Why can't I remember? How bizarre. Maybe Jai San can fill in the blanks later."

"How is she?" Lorne accepted the bone china cup and saucer from Angela after she had filled it with coffee served from a silver coffee pot. The aroma of the beans filled Lorne's nostrils, reminding her how foolish she had been as a child walking down the high street and detesting the smell wafting out of the Cawardines coffee shop.

"Jai San has gone into her shell. She gives the impression of being fine during the day—grateful to Anthony for the distraction, I suppose—but come the evening it's a different story. I see her out there wandering around the garden in a daze. My heart breaks in two, seeing her like that. I'm not sure I could switch off my feelings as well as she appears to."

"Poor thing. Does she speak much English?" Lorne asked before sipping her coffee.

"She gets by, and is improving daily. She constantly reads to Anthony; he loves stories, especially stories about King Arthur and Merlin. I think it also helps Jai San to learn the language. I give her the option of ringing home often so she doesn't feel cut off, but she says once a month is enough. I don't think she likes to take advantage."

"She sounds like a real sweetheart. I can't wait to meet her." Lorne hoped that Angela would take the hint that she was eager to meet the au pair, but she didn't. Lorne came to the conclusion that the wealthy woman was lonely and in need of stimulating conversation. "You say you work for a charity, Angela—do you mind me asking which one?"

Her smile broadened. "It's a new heart charity called Beating Life. I'm the founder of it. My father died of heart disease when I was in my teens, and I always promised that if I ever came into money, the first thing I'd do was to set up a charity to help those suffering from the same illness."

Lorne wondered what she meant by 'coming into money,' but felt asking the question would seem too rude. Then she remembered Jade telling her that Angela had recently married a wealthy man. Roger, wasn't it? That would explain her sudden wealth, but that was last year. Hadn't the butler said she'd bought and renovated this place five years ago? Curiosity got the better of her, "Came into money?"

"A long-lost aunt of mine left me this place in her will. Of course, it was a wreck when I took it over, but I didn't really mind. I saw it as a labour of love, creating this place. When I married Roger last year, it was on the proviso that we live here."

"I see. I don't blame you in the slightest. What does Roger do for a living?"

Her chest puffed out. "He's an accountant. He stays in London at his penthouse all week and returns home at the weekend."

Lorne found that snippet of information very odd, considering he had a small son of his own. Maybe he'd married Angela with the intention of her just being the boy's mother? She bit her tongue and didn't voice her concerns. "So with your husband working away and you busy most days with your charity, I can understand your need for employing an au pair. I admire you greatly for taking on another woman's child like that, I'm not sure I could do it."

Angela's brow furrowed slightly. "I've never really thought about it. I knew from the minute Roger and I started going out that he and Anthony came as a package; I didn't see it as a problem between us."

Lorne could see the glow in the woman's cheeks when she either spoke or thought about her husband. Looking around the room, Lorne spotted their wedding picture above the ornate fireplace. He seemed to be a likeable enough chap. He had thinning blond hair and youthful good looks. She could see the attraction, at a stretch. A very long stretch, he wasn't her type at all. "He seems a nice man," Lorne said.

"He's wonderful. I'm lucky to have him."

And he you, as you've taken on the responsibility of his son. Lorne drained the coffee in her cup and smiled at Angela. "Any chance I can have a quick chat with Jai San now? I hate to hurry things, but I'll have to be making a move soon."

"I've been twittering on, do forgive me." Instead of ringing a bell, as Lorne expected her to do, Angela left the room and came back with her arm wrapped around a tiny Asian girl's shoulders. "Lorne, this is our little treasure, Jai San."

The girl bowed her head and didn't look Lorne in the eye until she spoke. "Hello, Jai San. There's no need to be afraid. Is it all right if Jai San sits with us for a while?"

"Of course." Angela guided the girl to the other end of the sofa Lorne was sitting on and went back to her own seat.

Lorne moved to the seat next to Jai San. "There really is no need to worry. Do you mind if I ask you a few questions about your sister?"

Water filled eyes met Lorne's and her heart went out to her. Jai San nodded slowly.

"I'm sorry for your loss. It must have been a great shock to you."

"My baby sister was coming here for a better life...like me. Now she's gone."

Lorne reached for her hand and held it firmly in her own. "Can I ask how your sister came to be on that ship?"

"The lady at the agency arranged it."

Lorne looked over her shoulder at Angela, who quickly rose and left the room to find something. She came back seconds later and held out a business card for Lorne to take.

"Here you go—forgive my absentmindedness. This is the agency we contacted to employ Jai San."

"Ah, that's very helpful, thank you." Lorne sensed that Jai San was beginning to feel uncomfortable. She proceeded with caution. "How did you come to work for the agency?"

Jai San fidgeted in her seat for several minutes, and Lorne was about to ask the question again when the young woman's head lifted and their gazes met. "I met a man."

Lorne continued to smile at Jai San to put the girl at ease. "Where did you meet this man? In the UK?"

"Yes. I came here with three other girls. A man promised us a better life in England and gave us a lift in his boat." She fell silent until Lorne squeezed her hand to urge her to go on. "It was a trick. When we got here, he...he sold us."

"Sold you!" Angela cried out.

Lorne had suspected as much, so she wasn't as surprised as Angela by the revelation. She turned to see Angela shaking her head a look of disgust on her face. Lorne gave her a warning glance, hoping that Angela would restrain her emotions.

Jai San took a little coaxing to continue her woeful tale. Lorne felt the young girl was just on the edge of divulging valuable information when they heard a noise out in the hallway.

"Get out of my way, old man." The door to the lounge swung open, and in stomped Roger.

On a Thursday! Angela has already told me that Roger never comes home during the week. How odd, Lorne thought. The instant Jai San heard his voice out in the hallway, her grip tightened on Lorne's hand. Was that out of fear?

Angela bolted out of the chair and ran to greet him. "Roger! What are you doing here? Not that it isn't lovely to see you, of course, but you're not due home until tomorrow."

He gave his wife a half-smile and kissed her briefly on the lips before he walked over to where Lorne and Jai San were sitting. He held out his hand and introduced himself. "Roger North, and you are?"

Lorne shook his hand and noticed his shake was firm but clammy. Her father had drummed into her at the beginning of her police career that you could tell a lot from a man's handshake.

"Now, Roger, you naughty man, you know very well who this is; I told you Lorne was coming."

Lorne rose from her seat so he wasn't towering over her, and their gazes locked. She felt his eyes burning their way through hers. She was determined not to look away, to hold his stare until he broke contact.

Eventually, he turned to his wife. "That's right—I totally forgot. I had an appointment in the area and thought I'd drop in to surprise you, sweetheart."

Well, your gullible wife might believe that story, mate, but I'm afraid I don't. What have you got to hide? Lorne dropped down in her seat again and automatically reached for Jai San's hand, but the girl fought to pull her hand away, Lorne refused to give up, and eventually, the young girl let out an exasperated sigh and stopped struggling.

She watched Roger's reaction to the incident with interest. His eyes narrowed, but a slight smile remained on his face. Lorne glanced sideways and saw Jai San's head bowed, her focus lingering on a spot on the carpet in front of her. *There's something dodgy going on here, and I'm not liking it.*

"Please don't let me interrupt your conversation," Roger said.

Lorne, ever the suspicious type, regarded his tone as taunting.

It was Jai San who spoke next, in the quietest of voices. "I finished now."

Lorne felt the girl stiffen beside her, and she sensed that a barrier had been erected and it would be pointless to continue. Thinking she had enough information to go on already, Lorne decided to end the meeting. Roger was making her feel uncomfortable, anyway, and she sensed that Jai San was dying to get away from him, too. It bothered her that Angela didn't seem to pick up on the strain that had developed in the room the minute her husband had walked into it. *Was love really that blind?*

Lorne gently squeezed Jai San's hand before she released it. "Thank you for being so brave, Jai San. Again, I'm so sorry for your loss. You have my word that I will get the people concerned and take great pleasure in seeing them locked away for many years to come."

Roger made a noise in his throat, and Lorne immediately looked up at him. His eyebrows shot up questioningly. She bit back the sarcastic retort that was balancing precariously on the tip of her tongue and issued him a taut smile, instead. It irked Lorne that he seemed somehow triumphant that he'd interrupted their meeting.

"Jai San, you may go now," Roger said, dismissing the young girl. She left the room without making eye contact with anyone and closed the door gently behind her.

"Well, that was a revelation," Angela said as she flopped down in her chair.

Lorne refused to go over the details Jai San had confided in her in front of Roger and stood up, her intentions obvious. She was disappointed their meeting had been drawn to a close early, either intentionally or otherwise, by Angela's husband. To wipe the smug smile off his face she tried to bluff her way out of a frustrating and awkward situation. "She's given me some valuable information that will go a long way to solving this case. Thank you for your hospitality, Angela. It was a pleasure meeting you both. I'll be in touch with good news soon, I hope."

"You're not leaving on my account, are you?" Roger asked, a little too slyly for Lorne's liking.

"People to see and places to go, I'm afraid." Lorne held her hand out first to Angela and then to her husband before she left the room. She let out a huge sigh when she walked through the hallway toward the front door. Out of the corner of her eye, standing in an alcove, she saw Jai San. Lorne rushed over to her. The girl had tears streaming from her eyes. "Please help me get out of here. Please."

The words shocked Lorne. "I'll do everything in my power, Jai San. Hang in there. I'll be back for you soon."

CHAPTER TEN

"Katy will be here soon," Tony said. He approached her chair from behind, hooked an arm around under her chin, and kissed the top of her head. "I hate it when you're so quiet."

Lorne sighed. "I hate being quiet. It's nothing you've done, hon. I'm just thinking about the case. It's so frustrating."

"I know, but you know what they say about a problem shared. You know it's going to take a little time for things to slot into place on this one. Let's see what Katy has for us before we start getting downhearted and frustrated, huh?"

"You're right, as usual. I thought I'd make a lasagne for dinner— what do you think?"

He loosened his grip and sat at the table next to her. His eyes sparkled with delight. "I'd say I've died and gone to heaven. I love your lasagnes. Anything I can do to help?"

Knowing what her husband's knife skills and cooking abilities were like, she shook her head vigorously. "I'll be fine messing about in here on my own. If you're looking for a job, you could ring that agency for me. I forgot to ring them earlier and got distracted when the new arrivals turned up. See what you can find out about Jai San—discreetly, of course."

"On my way, if my efficient cooking skills aren't wanted around here," he said, pretending to be hurt.

Lorne watched him leave the room with a broad smile on her face. She really was the luckiest girl alive to have such a wonderful man by her side. She thought back to her life with her ex and an involuntary shudder coursed through her. *Enough of this. Get your arse in gear, girl.*

She was chopping the onions, tears spilling from her eyes, when Tony came back into the kitchen almost ten minutes later. "Any good?" She asked, pressing the tea towel into her eyes, hoping it would ease the stinging. It didn't; if anything, it only made things worse.

"Forget your own tip, did you?"

She poked her tongue out at him. "Go on."

"The owner was really cagey. She refused to answer any questions over the phone and repeatedly told me that she ran a legitimate business."

"Oh, did she now? Well, when people start ramming that down your throat, in my experience, the opposite is usually true. I'll see if Katy wants to pay the agency a visit with me over the weekend—an unofficial kind of visit if you like."

"Why don't you leave it until Monday, and we'll both go. Katy will be looking forward to her weekend off."

The back door opened midway through Tony's sentence. "Too bloody right I am."

Although Katy smiled when she spoke, Lorne noticed an angry glint in her eyes. She stepped forward and kissed Katy on both cheeks. "How lovely to see you. Tony, will you get Katy's bags for her, please?"

"Bags? That'll be one bag. I'm only staying the weekend, in case you've forgotten." Katy handed Tony the keys to her car. He gave her a welcome peck on the cheek and walked out the back door.

"Something wrong, love?" Lorne asked.

Her former partner sat down at the kitchen table and clenched her hands together in front of her. "I've had better days. I'm definitely looking forward to the weekend."

"Anything you want to talk about? I'm a good listener."

Katy smiled. "Correct that; you're the best listener around, Lorne. When I'm ready. Is that okay?"

"Of course it is—no pressure, you know that. Want to make yourself a coffee while I finish preparing the dinner?"

Tony stormed through the back door, carrying Katy's overnight bag in one hand and angrily waving the evening paper in the other. "Bloody idiot is going to get himself killed."

"What? Oh crap, is that Croft's story?"

"I only scanned through it, but the fool has named names and places. It's only a small story, but shit, it's going to do a hell of a lot of damage. Especially to him." Tony shook his head in disbelief.

"Do you think I should give him a ring?" Lorne asked, her mind racing.

"I'd leave it for today. We'll get in touch tomorrow."

"You're probably right—let things calm down a bit first. Okay, no more shop talk. We have a guest, and it's her birthday weekend."

Katy screwed up her nose. "Now, don't go treating me like royalty or anything. I'm just another year older, that's all."

Tony sniggered and went over to cuddle his wife. "Yeah, when you get to Lorne's age, you stop wanting to be reminded."

Lorne swiped him around the head. "I think you're forgetting one thing, matey: you're a couple of years older than me."

Katy laughed at the banter between them, and Lorne could sense the relief emanating from her. *Maybe she'll open up later and tell me what's going on. I hope her damn ex isn't causing her any grief.*

The evening ended up being a blast. Her father joined them and started to regale them with numerous funny incidents that had happened during his time as a DCI in the Met. They washed down Lorne's sumptuous lasagne with three bottles of special red that eagle-eyed Tony had seen in the bargain bin at Oddbins in the High Street.

At the end of the evening, Lorne showed Katy to her room. Before closing the door, she asked, "Feel up to talking yet?"

"Thanks for a wonderful evening, Lorne. I'd rather not spoil it, if you don't mind. I promise I'll tell you tomorrow. What do you have planned?"

Lorne shuffled her feet. "Umm...well, I thought we'd pay a few people a visit, if that's all right with you. I'll fill you in on what I've found out this week on the way."

"Yep, sounds great to me. Thanks again for tonight; I appreciated it. You all really made me feel part of the family."

"Never doubt that, Katy. You are—and always will be—part of our family. Goodnight, hon."

"Goodnight."

* * *

First thing the following morning, Lorne tried to ring Croft but couldn't get a reply. Worried, she hurriedly threw a breakfast together for all of them, then jumped in the car with Katy and set off for Croft's flat.

"Did you sleep well, Katy?"

"Like a log. Why is that? I haven't slept well in months now, and yet one night at your place, and I'm down for the count all night."

"Several contributing factors, I suspect. You were relaxed, several glasses of wine, and good company. Oh, and I suspect that's the first time in months you haven't had any stress to deal with, either." Lorne glanced sideways and saw the grin on Katy's face. "What's that look for?"

"You know me so well."

"Well enough to know when something major is troubling you. Is that ex hanging around again?" Katy turned to gaze out the window at the open fields whizzing past. "Katy?"

"Okay, you asked. Yesterday, I was suspended."

Lorne's head snapped around. The blast of a horn made her promptly turn back to face the road ahead. "What? Why? I can't believe Roberts would do such a thing!"

"He had little choice, really. I decked a suspect when I brought him in for questioning."

"You decked him?"

"The bloody toe-rag touched me up when I took him through to the holding cell. I smacked him in the mouth and he cried out, turned 'round, and slammed his face into the wall to maximize the damage."

"Compo claim, you reckon?"

"Yeah, he's an old hand at it, or so the desk sergeant said. It doesn't alter the fact that I struck him. That part was caught on the camera, but him flinging himself at the wall wasn't. I'd do it again in a heartbeat. Damn bastard had no right copping a feel like that. Yuck! It makes my skin crawl just thinking about it. What about *my* rights in all this? Roberts said he had little option but to suspend me until the enquiry takes place in a few weeks."

"You're on full pay, though, right?"

"Yeah, why?"

Lorne smiled. "Come work with us. At least see how things work out during your suspension. I'd love to team up with you again. The only thing is, we couldn't afford to pay you much."

Katy twisted in her seat to face her. "Really? To be honest, I don't give a shit about the money side of things. Though, thinking logically about this, I have rent to pay on my crappy flat."

"No problem on that front, either—move in with us."

"Whoa! Slow down a minute. Is Tony all right with this? Is your father?"

"They will be," Lorne mumbled sheepishly.

Katy remained quiet for a good few minutes, mulling over the plan. "If the others are agreeable, I'd *love* to do it. Can we have an honest and open discussion about it this evening?"

Lorne's hand left the steering wheel and found Katy's. "You're on. God, it's going to be so cool working with you again."

"It'll be like old times. The only thing that'll be different is I'll be a year older," Katy grumbled under her breath.

Lorne laughed as she pulled up outside the block of flats where Croft lived. She and Katy got out of the car, and Lorne scanned the area for Croft's vehicle. "As I suspected, it's probably in the garage for repair."

Katy raised a questioning eyebrow. "Meaning?"

"Sorry, I was going to fill you in on what happened outside the wine bar the other night, but our conversation veered off in a whole different direction. I'll tell you on the way back. Tony and I had the scare of our lives."

Lorne led the way up the narrow path and into the reception area, which was surprisingly open to the public. Graffiti lined the walls and the stench of urine filled their nostrils as they made their way up two flights of stairs to the next level. "Ah, number three, here it is." Lorne gave the door four sharp knocks and waited. When there was no response, she crouched down and peeped through the letterbox. Looking along the tiny dark hallway didn't give any clues as to whether Croft was at home or not. She stood up and knocked again, then turned back to Katy. "I couldn't see anything. If the lounge is at the end of the hallway, the door is shut. If he doesn't answer this time, we'll leave."

"Can you call his mobile?" Katy glanced around, seemingly uncomfortable.

"Good idea." Lorne took out her mobile and the slip of paper she'd written Croft's address and phone number down on and punched in the number.

Katy bent down to the letterbox and placed her ear up against it. "The phone's ringing inside."

"It is? That's strange." Lorne watched as Katy stood up, took three steps back towards the half brick wall that formed the balcony, and ran at the front door. "Katy, what the f—"

"Help me get in there. I'm sure I just heard a groan."

"Damn." Lorne shouldered the door while Katy ran at it again and kicked it. The door flew open, splintering the doorframe in the process. They both ran down the narrow hall to the door at the end. Lorne stood in the doorway and stared at Croft groaning and wriggling around on the frayed carpet in the lounge. Katy quickly rushed past her to get to Croft.

"Keep still. We'll get an ambulance." Katy looked up at Lorne, expecting her to place the call, then began checking Croft's injuries.

Lorne stepped outside the flat and rang 9-9-9. After giving the woman the address, she pleaded, "Please hurry. We urgently need an ambulance—a man has been badly beaten. Yes…I'd say his life is in imminent danger. Okay, quick as you can." She hung up and ran back inside.

"They'll be here in around five minutes. How's he looking, Katy?"

"I've tried to stop the bleeding from his stomach, but he's already lost a significant amount of blood."

Lorne winced and gagged a little when she noticed that half the fingers of Croft's right hand had been cut off and were lying on the carpet beside him. "Derek, why didn't you listen to me?" she said under her breath, not expecting him to hear her. Lorne asked Katy, "Is there anything I can do?"

Lorne was thankful that Katy had taken control of the situation. She would have struggled to remember her first aid training.

"Get me some towels to help stop the bleeding to his stomach, and maybe a tea towel or a small towel to wrap around his hand. Also, try to find some ice or a bag of peas and a plastic bag to put his fingers in; maybe the hospital will be able to sew them back on."

Lorne left the room and returned a few seconds later, she gave Katy two hand towels. Katy bent down and gently bandaged Croft's bloody, mutilated hand in the tea towel.

Thankfully, in the distance, they heard the ambulance's siren growing louder. Lorne rushed back outside and leaned over the wall. As the ambulance turned into the road, she waved frantically at the driver, who flashed his lights letting her know he'd seen her. She remained on the landing and watched the paramedics open up the rear of their vehicle and extract a stretcher. Both men joined her on the balcony outside Croft's flat a few moments later, sounding out of breath.

"He's through here." She showed them into the lounge. When the two paramedics marched into the room, Katy left Croft's side.

"You've done a good job, miss. Well done," the younger, dark haired paramedic said, smiling at Katy.

Katy appeared shell-shocked, as if sapped of all her energy, and merely nodded in return. Lorne threw an arm around her shoulder and hugged her. "You all right?"

"I think so. Poor bloke. This could go either way, Lorne, with the amount of blood he's lost. I'd better call it in."

"Crap, how can you? You're supposed to be suspended, remember? I'll do it." Lorne rang the station directly. They assured her that two officers would be sent to the address ASAP. "You'd better wait in the car. I don't want them seeing you here. I have a legitimate reason for being here, but you haven't." She handed Katy the keys to her father's Nova. The paramedics hoisted Croft gently onto the stretcher, and when they strapped him in, he cried out in pain. The younger paramedic gave him an injection that instantly calmed him down. *I could do with a shot of that, myself.* Lorne held the front door open and watched the group head down the stairs to the ambulance. She ran back in the lounge and started hunting around, looking for any clues as to who had attacked Croft, but found nothing. She had an inkling of who had carried out the assault, but it would have simplified things if she had found a print or two.

While she waited for the police to arrive, Lorne rang Tony to tell him what had happened.

"Jesus. I want you out of there this instant, no arguments. Just get out and come home."

"Tony, calm down! You know full well I'm not about to do that. Once the police have taken a statement, Katy and I will be heading over to the hospital to see what Croft's prognosis is. Then I'm going to drop in on the agency, and *then* we'll come home."

"Your stubbornness is going to get you into serious trouble one of these days, oh wife of mine," he growled uncharacteristically down the phone.

Suitably chastised, Lorne hung up just as someone knocked on the front door.

Two plain clothed CID officers looked quizzically at her when she opened the door to let them in. "Lorne? What are you doing here?" asked Des Taylor, whom she had known for years.

Clearing her throat, she invited them in and showed them into the lounge. "I'm a private investigator now, Des. I've been working on a case with the gentleman who owns this flat. I hadn't heard from him for a day or two. I was worried, and decided to call 'round to see if everything was all right. When I arrived, I rang the bell, but Croft didn't answer. I called his mobile and heard it ringing, so I presumed he was inside the flat. I looked through the letterbox and heard Croft moaning. I thought he needed help, so I broke down the door to gain access."

The other copper looked back over his shoulder at the front door and then turned to face Lorne again. "I'm impressed that you did that all by yourself wearing those heels." His tone was one of condescension.

She had never liked the idiot. She'd tolerated him during her time on the force, but had never liked him. "That's right, Miller. I might have left the Met, but I haven't lost my touch."

He looked at her, shook his head in disbelief, and took out his notebook. Before the idiot copper could ask a question, Des said, "So, what happened, Lorne?"

"After I broke down the door, I found Derek Croft lying in here on the floor." She pointed to the patch of blood which she hoped would back up her statement. "The paramedics whisked him away."

"Which hospital?" Miller asked, getting ready to write her answer down.

"St. Thomas's."

Des surveyed the bloody area and then looked up at Lorne. "He was in pretty bad shape, I take it. Did he manage to tell you what went on?"

"No. He'd lost a lot of blood by the time I'd got here. He had an open wound in his stomach, and the fingers on his right hand had been cut off."

"Why?" Miller demanded.

Lorne eyed him with displeasure. "Why what?"

Miller tutted. "Why were his fingers cut off?"

"Er...I don't know, let me think." She placed her finger on her chin, much to Des's amusement. Then she sarcastically told Miller, "Maybe it's because he's a journalist. You want me to do your job for you?"

"I'm not with you," Miller looked confused.

Lorne turned to Des for help. He shrugged his shoulders and said, "You see what I have to put up with? Miller, get a grip. If he ain't got any fingers, he can't write his damn stories, can he? Leave your brains at home today, did you?"

"All right, Des, there's no need for that." He held the side of his face. "You know my wisdom tooth is playing up."

"Yeah, yeah. I gave you sympathy in the car on the way over here, there's no need to milk it."

Lorne had to stifle a chuckle at the comedy double act, and was reminded of her days working alongside Pete. Boy, did she miss him. She glanced at her watch. "You boys mind hurrying things along?"

Miller nodded his head in her direction. "Get her, Mrs. I'm Very Busy P.I."

"Shut up, Miller. Sorry, Lorne. Anything else you can tell us?"

"Not much, really. I want to get over to the hospital to see how Derek is. I think you'll find that the case is already being investigated by your lot. Not that you've come up with much yet."

"We'll look into it when we get back. No point asking if you found any prints or a weapon while you were waiting for us, I suppose."

"Nope, nothing. Whoever attacked Derek was thorough. I'd even go as far to say they were pros."

"A professional hit man?" Miller asked.

"Yep, looked that way to me. Here's my card. Can you do me a favour and give me a call if you find out anything?" She handed the card to Des.

He took it and nodded. "Sure thing. Thanks for hanging around. We'll get the Scene of Crime Officers to go over the place. If they find anything, I'll let you know."

Miller turned his head sharply in his partner's direction. "We will?"

"Yeah, Miller, we will. Lorne's one of the good guys. You see, we help out the good guys because you never know when you might need them."

Lorne bid the two of them farewell and contemplated as she made her way down to the car to join Katy. Getting in the car, she told Katy, "Sometimes—just sometimes—I find myself shaking my head, wondering how some guys get into the Met. There are some real dickheads chasing down criminals nowadays." She hit the steering wheel with the heel of her hand. "Christ, it's no wonder crime is escalating in the London area."

Katy chuckled and raised an eyebrow. "I'll tell you why that is, Ms. Simpkins—'cause you're no longer with the Met. There was a time, not too long ago, when as soon as a criminal heard your name mentioned, they knew their number was up."

Lorne shook her head vehemently. "Don't be daft. Hey, with guys like Miller guarding our streets, I'll tell you this: the bloody criminals are rubbing their hands every second of every day. Five minutes in a room with him, and I'm very confident of that. What an arsehole! I feel sorry for Des; the weight of responsibility on his shoulders at the end of the day must be horrendous."

"We all have our crosses to bear. Where to now?"

"If it's all right with you, I'd like to go to the hospital, maybe hang around a while until Croft is able to talk to us."

Katy shrugged. "Whatever, I've got nothing else planned."

Lorne winced at the undeniable dig. "Ouch! Sorry, Katy. I know it's your birthday tomorrow, and this is the last thing you want to be doing this weekend, but…"

"It was a joke, Lorne, lighten up. Sometimes you're too serious for words."

Lorne glanced at her and decided that Katy was upset about the situation, but like a true friend, she was willing to put her feelings aside for the sake of the case.

CHAPTER ELEVEN

"I'm watching them now, boss."

"Take a photo on your phone and get back here ASAP. I wanna know who this bitch is. What car is she driving?" Sly Sansom asked.

The guy in the black four-by-four sniggered. "A roller skate of a car. Think it's a Nova or something like that. I could finish the job now, if you like. This baby would crush that piece of shite in no time at all."

"Hold tight, big man. Let's see what she knows first. You did a good job on Croft. It might serve as a warning for her to keep her nose out."

"Righto, boss. I got a pic of her before she got in the roller skate. I'm on my way back to base now."

Sansom ended the call and instantly dialled another number.

"It's me. My boys have silenced that reporter once and for all."

"What? They've killed him?"

Sansom cringed at the anger in the other man's voice. Maybe he'd misunderstood his instructions. 'Shut Croft up' was what he'd said. Tentatively, he told his boss, "Not quite. They sliced a few of his fingers off and knocked him around a little." He listened in dread as his boss let out a long sigh.

"I'm working with fucking idiots. If he didn't have the police involved in this already, they will be now, you *prick*. Suspicious injuries are always reported when someone is admitted to hospital. Don't you know that? How fucking long have you been in this game? Two fucking minutes, by the look of things."

"Sorry, boss. I didn't think of that," Sansom mumbled in response.

"That's blatantly obvious, dickhead. When's the next shipment due? Let's hope there's no cock-ups with this one, eh?"

He brightened up and smiled. "Because of the ship going down, I've arranged another shipment as soon as poss, the next one is due in tomorrow evening. Thirty girls will be arriving to replace the others."

"Good, glad to hear that you're capable of doing something right."

* * *

Accident and Emergency was fairly quiet when Lorne and Katy arrived. Lorne walked up to the chubby blonde girl at reception. "Hi, I'd like to be kept informed of Mr. Croft's status, if that's all right?"

The blonde smiled up at her and then looked down at the paperwork on her desk. "Are you family?"

Lorne's mouth turned down. "He has no family; they were all killed in a plane crash last year. I'm the closest thing he's got now. I'm a family friend. We're very close."

"Oh, that's such a shame. Of course. Why don't you take a seat over there? I'll get word to the doctor as soon as I can."

Katy was already sitting where the receptionist had pointed, and Lorne joined her. "I think we could be in for a long wait."

"That figures. Are they going to tell you how he's getting on?" Katy sounded surprised.

"Yeah, I told her a white lie. I said his relatives were killed last year and I'm the closest thing he's got to family now."

"You little minx."

"Not really. There's method to my madness. For all I know, he's probably got family, but the last thing I want to do is put them in any kind of danger. I'm sure Derek would feel the same way. I doubt he'd want his family mixed up in this; that's my guess, anyway."

"You're right. I know I wouldn't want anyone I loved anywhere near this. You think whoever did this is going to come back and finish the job?" Katy asked, lowering her voice so the people opposite couldn't hear their conversation.

Lorne whispered back, "I'm not sure. They might. If Derek comes out of this alive, he'll be even more determined to shut this operation down—that's what I'm really worried about."

They chatted on and off for the next few hours until a doctor came by to speak to them. "Follow me, please." The tall doctor in his mid to late-thirties led them into the family room a few feet away. "This is a little out of my comfort zone to be talking to you, especially as you're not Mr. Croft's immediate family."

"I understand, Doctor. But I'm really all he has. Can I ask what the prognosis is?"

"The short answer is that he'll survive. We won't know if the surgery to sew his fingers back on was a success or not, it remains to be seen if they'll be fully functional again, we won't know until he wakes up. We patched up the wound to his stomach which wasn't as bad as it had first appeared. Thankfully, all his vital organs were missed. He has a fracture in his right cheekbone. We'll have to see how much damage has been done after the swelling has gone down."

"I see. Is he awake? Can we see him?" Lorne asked.

"You can see him for a brief moment. Have the police been informed of the attack?"

"Oh, yes. I stayed behind to speak to them while the ambulance brought Derek in. Not sure if they'll catch the bastards who did this, though."

"Thank you—that saves me informing them. I'll take you up to the ward now. We've put him in a private room. I imagine that he'll still be unconscious."

"That's okay. He might sense us being there and come 'round. Is there any form of security on the ward?"

The doctor turned and studied her in surprise. "In an NHS hospital?"

"I know, I know. I thought it might be worth asking."

"Why would you ask such a question? Do you think the people who beat Mr. Croft up will turn up here?"

Lorne shrugged. "I'm not sure. However, I think we should be aware of the possibility."

They entered the lift and rode up to the next floor. After they exited the steel doors, the doctor said, "I don't like the sound of that. I'd hate for my staff to be put in any kind of danger. The board of governors wouldn't appreciate it either."

Lorne smiled to reassure him. "I'm sure it won't come to that, but I just wanted to make you aware of the situation. Maybe if you have any security guards on the premises, one of them could patrol Croft's ward now and then—you know, to act as a deterrent."

"Hmm," the doctor mumbled, sounding none too happy with what she'd just told him. He pushed open the door to a private ward and allowed Lorne and Katy to enter the room before him.

Croft's eyes were firmly closed. His face was puffy, and his right eye was a rainbow of colours. A thick bandage covered one of his hands and a drip was connected to his left wrist. Lorne stepped towards the bed and gently touched his arm. "Derek, can you hear me?"

"He'll probably be out for hours yet," the doctor reminded her.

They heard a slight groan, and Derek Croft inched an eye open to look at them. He swallowed several times until he'd moistened his mouth enough to speak. "Lorne, is that you?"

"Glad to see you awake, matey. Can you tell us what happened? Who did this to you?"

He shook his head fractionally from side to side, but the pain proved to be too much for him, and wincing, he whispered, "No idea. I think there were two of them...but I'm not one hundred percent certain. They jumped me outside the flat—everything's a blur, really." He glanced down at his bandaged hand and looked up at her questioningly.

"It's all right, Derek, the doc here has done a fabulous job. You'll be able to use your hand again for work," Lorne assured him. She could feel the doctor's eyes boring into the back of her head and she turned to smile at him. His eyes rose to the ceiling; he looked annoyed with her for misinforming his patient. But she could hardly tell him the truth. What kind of wakeup message would that be?

All of a sudden, his good eye fluttered shut and he fell back to sleep again.

"I think you'd better leave him to rest now." He led them out of the room. "I hope your words don't come back and bite you somewhere painful. I told you the jury was still out with regard to whether he'll be able to use his hand again or not. I don't agree with giving my patients false hope."

"I'm sorry. Can you ring me when he wakes up properly? He might remember more then."

"Give your number to the ward sister. I'm far too busy to contact you personally." He turned on his heel and walked away from them down the echoing hallway.

Katy gently laughed. "Wow, that told you, didn't it?"

"Hey, I can do without your wise-arse comments, young lady. Come on, I'll give my number to the ward sister and then we'll try and get a hold of someone at the agency."

Katy looked at her watch. "It's almost five on a Saturday afternoon. I doubt they'll be around now."

"We'll give it a try anyway." She handed a business card to the sister, who tucked it away safely in a desk drawer. Lorne and Katy left the hospital.

"Aren't you going to ring first?" Katy asked as Lorne pulled out of the car park.

"No, I thought I'd surprise her. It's only ten minutes up the road, and—" She was interrupted by her mobile ringing. She hit the button on the hands-free. "Hello, Tom, what's up?" She was surprised to hear from her ex, as he didn't contact her much these days—not unless there was a problem with Charlie.

He came straight to the point. "Is Charlie with you?"

Lorne's stomach wrapped itself in knots. "You're kidding, right?"

"Do I sound as if I'm joking, Lorne? Christ, just answer the bloody question, will you?"

"Hey, listen, Tom, don't start getting shirty with me. Isn't Charlie supposed to be staying at a friend's house tonight?" Lorne brought the car to a halt at the side of the road amidst blasts of numerous of car horns. She gave the finger to the passing irate drivers.

"Yeah. She left her shoes here, and I rang her friend's house to say I'd drop them 'round, but her friend said she wasn't there."

"What do you mean she wasn't there? She hadn't arrived yet, or she had no intention of turning up there this weekend?"

"Her friend said she was supposed to be there, but Charlie cancelled on Thursday, told her she'd made arrangements to go out with you over the weekend."

Lorne let out an exasperated breath. "So it was planned. Has she been misbehaving at home lately? I told you to keep me informed if her character altered at all. It was the one thing the shrink told us to keep an eye on."

"It hasn't. She's been as good as gold for months now. Otherwise, I would have informed you, as per *your* instructions."

Lorne ignored the sarcasm in his tone. Even with their daughter missing, he was still goading her for an argument. *Sod you, Tom!*

"Well, give me some kind of clue, Tom, for Christ's sake. Does she have a new boyfriend? A new friend she's been going on about lately?"

"Not that I know of."

She could imagine him shrugging his shoulders and putting on a hopeless face, and it made her heart pump harder and faster. "Have you been neglecting her in favour of that new girlfriend of yours? Charlie told me how besotted you were with her."

"Piss off, Lorne. That's got nothing to do with you or why Charlie has gone missing."

"Really? You're certain of that, are you? You can be so naïve at times."

"Like I said already, piss off, Lorne. I've sacrificed everything— and I mean *everything*—for that girl. What exactly have you done for her? Except put her life in danger, that is."

An unintentional heavy breath escaped her lips before she responded, "Change the damn record, Tom. I'm surprised it hasn't been scratched to buggery by now."

Lorne saw Katy fidget in the passenger seat beside her and mouthed an apology. Katy whispered, "Arguing won't find Charlie any sooner. What time did she leave home?"

Before Tom had the chance to answer Lorne demanded, "What time did she leave home?"

"What? Oh, about two hours ago."

"Okay, I apologise for having a go at you. I have Katy here with me now; I'll get her to ring the station to ask the patrol cars to look out for Charlie. Don't go out, Tom—just stay there in case Charlie comes home. I'll ring you if we hear anything."

"Thanks," was all he said before he hung up.

Katy's mouth turned down. "I'm suspended, remember?"

"Damn. I'll ring Roberts myself, see if he'll help me out. But that'll have to wait until after I ring Tony, maybe she's turned up there."

She dialled her home number and waited. The phone rang non-stop, and just before it went into answerphone, a breathless Tony picked up. "Hello?"

"You took your time," she snapped at him uncharacteristically, immediately biting down on her lip in regret.

"One of the new pups was ill. I was outside checking on him. How did it go?"

"With Croft? He's in hospital—"

"What?" Tony exclaimed, interrupting her.

"Mind if I fill you in later? Charlie has gone missing and I'm scared."

"What? Isn't she supposed to be staying at a friend's house this weekend?"

"Yeah, but she hasn't turned up. Tom's just rung me."

"Okay, I know what you're like about Charlie; I'm sure it's nothing. Don't go getting yourself worked up into a state. Is there anything I can do?"

"Tell Dad for me and stay by the phone in case she rings. It's just that the last time—"

"Stop it. Let's not even think about that, all right? She's getting on for sixteen now, she'll be testing the water to see how far she can push you and Tom. And Lorne?"

"Yeah?"

"Don't even think of connecting her to this case. It's a coincidence—a bizarre coincidence. Until you have evidence to the contrary, don't waste your energy going down that route, okay?"

She expelled the breath she'd been holding in. Tony was right, he usually was. But it would never quell the niggling doubt she had worming its way into her stomach. Coincidence or not, the Unicorn's vile face tormented her. She threw open her car door and vomited in the curb. Closing the door again, she took a tissue from Katy and wiped her mouth.

"Lorne? Are you there?" Tony asked.

"Yeah, I'm here. Look, Katy and I are going to search around for a bit. I'll contact the station to ask them to keep an eye open for her. Ring me if she turns up, okay?"

"Of course I will."

"I'll ring later to let you know how we're doing."

"Okay. Hang in there. I love you."

"Love you, too."

She hung up and immediately rang Sean Roberts. "Sean, it's Lorne. Sorry—haven't got time for niceties; I need a favour."

"Shoot. If I can help, you know I will."

"Charlie's gone missing, and I need the boys on the beat to keep an eye out for her."

"What do you mean *missing*?"

"She was due at a friend's house for the weekend, but she hasn't shown up."

"I thought she stayed with you at the weekend."

Annoyed that he was delaying her getting on with the search, she snapped, "Ordinarily she does; however, she made other plans for this weekend. Sean, will you help or not? Katy and I are about to start driving around to see if we can find her, but the more people we have on the lookout, the better. If you're not willing to help, please tell me now and stop wasting my time."

"How to win friends and influence people the Lorne Simpkins way. Just kidding, before you snap my head off again. I'll get the guys to keep an eye out for her. Do you have an up-to-date photo of Charlie?"

"Hold on." She scrolled through the pictures on her phone and stopped at one of Charlie working in the kennels that she'd taken the previous weekend, then said, "Got one. Shall I send it to you?"

"Yep, send it through. I'll print it off and get the desk sergeant to distribute it to the lads. And what's all this about Katy being with you?"

Me and my big mouth. "It's her birthday this weekend—nice timing on the suspension, by the way. I told her to spend the weekend with us. I hadn't anticipated all this excitement when I suggested it, though."

"Charlie going missing, you mean?"

"Yeah, amongst other things. You know I'm investigating the trafficking case, don't you? Well, the criminals involved have just upped the ante. Once I know Charlie is safe, Katy and I will go hell for leather tracking this gang down."

Sean sighed deeply before he replied, "Katy is a serving officer in the Met; she cannot be involved in this case, Lorne. Do you hear me?"

"Loud and clear, Sean. So reinstate her or let her go."

"It's not as easy as that and you know it."

"It's as easy as you want it to be, Sean. It's time to show the Met what you're made of. Either stick up for one of the best serving officers you have, or lose her. I'd offer her a job in a heartbeat."

Another heavy sigh. "Send over the picture of Charlie and I'll see what I can do with regard to both matters. I promise. Ring me if you need anything else."

"I might take you up on that. Let me find Charlie first, and I'll get back to you with what developments I have on the case. It would be good to get some help on this one rather than come up against a brick wall, as Katy has." There she went again, dropping Katy in the shit.

She heard Katy tut, and turning, she mouthed an apology. Katy gave her a brief nod and glanced out the windscreen again.

"I'll pretend I didn't hear that, Lorne. I'll be in touch if we find out anything. You do the same if Charlie turns up, yes?"

"Sure thing. Thanks, Sean."

She hung up, sent the picture through to Sean and then pulled away in a gap in the traffic. "Sorry, Katy."

"No worries. Where are we going to look first?"

"I thought I'd drive around the park where Charlie and her friends used to hang out. I'm out of touch what her favourite haunts are now, and there's no point in asking Tom, I doubt he'd know. Damn…why haven't I taken more interest in her friends lately?"

"Hey, you can pack that in. I'm not going to listen to you droning on, blaming yourself."

"Reprimand accepted and appreciated, thank you."

For the next hour or so, they drove around the area closest to Tom and Charlie's home, but drew a blank. They were just about to set off on foot to ask the cashiers in the local shops if they had seen Charlie when Sean Roberts rang.

"Here's our initial findings: we managed to track down a few of Charlie's friends. At first they were reluctant to speak to the uniformed coppers, but after a few idle threats, they finally told the officers that your daughter was seen getting into a car—"

"Oh my God! Not again, *please* not again." They were lucky Lorne had pulled the car over to the curb; she dreaded to think what would have happened had she still been driving.

"Now, Lorne, hear me out. The kids said the car belonged to her new boyfriend. Any ideas who he is?"

She shook her head, as if he was sitting beside her in the car. Katy elbowed her in the ribs. "Sorry, Sean. I had no idea she had a boyfriend. The question is why she felt the need to keep him a secret."

"Not sure. The kids didn't seem to know she had one, either, if that helps."

"So it might be a new boyfriend, but then again, it might not?" she asked, confused.

"Look, I'm just passing on what I know. I hoped it might put your mind at ease a little."

"Thanks, Sean, it's appreciated."

They ended the call. Lorne punched the steering wheel a few times and then plucked up the courage to ring Tom back.

"It's me, and no, we haven't found her yet."

"Christ, it's been hours. Where the hell is she?"

Lorne detected the anxiety in his tone and almost pulled out of asking the question. "Tom, has Charlie said anything to you about having a boyfriend?"

"No! Why?"

"She was last seen getting into a car with a lad."

"Shit! She hasn't told me anything. Hasn't she mentioned it to you in one of your mother and daughter chats?"

Here comes the part where he lays the blame firmly at my door.

"No, Tom, she hasn't. Okay, I'm hanging up now so I can continue looking. I'll keep you up to date." She hung up and said to Katy, "Why the heck do I bother? I know he thinks I'm a shit mother. Every opportunity he gets, he takes pleasure in flinging it down my throat."

"What did he say?"

"Nothing much, but I could tell by the tone of his voice that the inference was there. Agh…he's such an arsehole."

"Yeah, and you're well rid of him. Concentrate on finding Charlie. I have a plan—want to hear it?"

"Of course."

Katy had a smug look on her face. "Think back to when you were a kid, in your teens, and you had a new boyfriend—what did you do?"

"Not applicable, I'm afraid; the only two men I was involved with in my teens were Sean Roberts, who was a workaholic, and boring Tom, whose idea of a cracking night out was spending hours down at his local pub playing on the one-armed bandits."

"Yikes, and you went on to marry him?"

"Yeah, I also went on to regret it and got a divorce eventually. What are you getting at, anyway?" she asked, desperate to change the subject.

"We're in the big city. If he's just bought his car, he'll be desperate to show it off."

"Crap, don't tell me that—my nerves are frayed enough as it is."

"Listen. Youngsters never think of saving their petrol, so my guess is he's heading into London to show her the sights."

Lorne contemplated Katy's idea for a few minutes. "You could have something there. Let's go! We've wasted enough time around here."

CHAPTER TWELVE

"Charlie and I went up on that last year; made me quite sick, but I didn't tell her that," Lorne told Katy as they drove past the London Eye. "I doubt they'd be on there—too expensive for kids. They'll be looking for cheap thrills. Are there such things in this tourist magnet of a city?" She wracked her brains, trying to come up with anything, and drew another blank. It was pointless asking Katy, as she was a northerner and she hadn't been stationed in London long enough to have got caught up in the tourist trap.

"Not something I'd relish going on. I haven't got a clue about the cost of some of the attractions. Hey, they wouldn't necessarily be visiting these places as such—driving past them, yes, but not actually visiting them. Let's carry on to the next one. We're beginning to lose the light now. I don't suppose Roberts hinted at what kind of car this kid had?"

"No, and I forgot to ask. Dumb of me, right?"

"You're too harsh on yourself, Lorne. Just stop it. All this negativity isn't getting the job done any better."

"Who made you the smart kid on the block?" she said playfully.

"What about Buck House?"

"That's miles from here, but doable. I'll sweep past some other touristy places on the way. Good thinking."

The sun lit up the evening sky in scorching red tones. Any other time, Lorne would have pulled the car over and marvelled at the wonderful sight. There was something special about sunsets and sunrises that touched her heart and made her think what a beautiful place the world was. Not today, though—not with Charlie on the missing list.

In the middle of negotiating the rush hour traffic at a roundabout, her mobile rang. "Katy, do you mind getting that for me?" she asked.

"Hello? Just a minute." Katy covered the phone's mouthpiece and motioned for Lorne to take it.

"Put it in the hands-free contraption, would you? Who is it?"

"Roberts," Katy replied as she fastened the phone in position on the dashboard.

"Sean, hi. Have you found out anything?" Lorne drew in an anticipated breath.

"I take it you're driving, Lorne. I need you to stop the car."

Her hands took on a life of their own and began to shake on the steering wheel. She indicated, pulled the car to a halt, and switched off the engine.

"Okay, the car is stationary. You're scaring me shitless, Sean. What's going on?"

"We think we've located the vehicle—"

"But that's wonderful news, isn't it?" She turned to Katy and held her crossed fingers up in front of her.

"Umm…not exactly. It was found overturned and on fire."

"Oh no! Please don't tell me that. Did they get out? Was Charlie in the car?"

Sean sighed heavily. "She was there, and yes, the fire brigade managed to get them out—"

"Tell me where."

"Down near the Embankment."

Lorne started the car, but Katy's hand clasped her arm. "I'll drive," Katy said, her tone one of authority. Katy opened the passenger's door and ordered Lorne to move over into the passenger's seat while she ran around the front of the car and jumped in the driver's seat.

"They're still at the scene, Lorne. When you get there, for heaven's sake let them get on with their jobs. You hear me?" Sean insisted.

"Fine. Don't worry. Anything else?" she asked, exasperated that he knew her so well.

"No. Just be careful getting there."

His extended hesitation concerned her. She glanced over at Katy. "Quick, put your foot down."

They arrived at the scene within ten minutes. Both women sprinted from the car. However, two uniformed policemen blocked their path. "Please stand back. There's nothing to see here, ladies."

Lorne pointed at the upturned car and screeched, "My daughter was in that car."

The coppers looked at each other flummoxed by her outburst. Finally, Katy shouted, "Let us through, you idiots, I'm a DS in the Met."

Shamefaced, the coppers held the crime scene tape up. Lorne and Katy rushed past them and over to the ambulance situated far enough away from the flaming car to be out of any danger.

Two paramedics were about to strap Charlie into a stretcher. Her neck was encased in a collar and a man in biker's leathers was at her side.

"Charlie? Can you hear me?" Lorne clutched her daughter's hand in her own as tears slid down her cheeks.

"Are you the girl's mother?" the man in leathers asked.

"She is, and you are?" Katy replied for Lorne.

"I'm the emergency doctor. I've sedated her. She's in a sorry state, I'm afraid, but at least she's alive." He looked over his shoulder and nodded at the body lying under a white sheet. "The same can't be said for her companion."

"How badly hurt is she, Doctor?" Katy asked.

"Your daughter was thrown from the car. She was unconscious when we arrived. It's precautionary to put the neck brace on. I'm afraid we won't know more until we get her to the hospital. Bearing in mind what happened to the driver, I think your daughter is an extremely lucky girl. I don't want to give you false hope, though, so let's wait and see."

Lorne gasped and Katy placed a soothing hand on her back. "She's only sixteen," Lorne whispered.

"We like to think positively about things, Doctor. I know you and the hospital will do your best," Katy said.

The doctor nodded. One of the paramedics gave the thumbs-up. "We're good to go, doc."

Katy pulled Lorne aside so the paramedics could load the stretcher into the back of the ambulance. "Do you want to travel with her?"

"Go on. I'll follow on in the car," Katy told her with a half-smile.

"I'd like that, thanks. Damn, what about ringing Tom and Tony?" Lorne faltered as she followed the stretcher into the ambulance.

"Leave it to me. I'll ring Tony and he can contact Tom." Katy turned back to the doctor and asked, "Which hospital are they taking her to?"

"It'll be St. Thomas's. We'd better get going."

As the door closed to the ambulance Lorne shouted to Katy, "See you there, and drive carefully."

In shock, she looked down at her injured daughter, and all the personal regrets she'd had of putting her career before motherhood came flooding back with a suffocating vengeance. Lorne's breath was coming in short, sharp bursts, and the air in the ambulance seemed to be disappearing faster than a rocket being launched into space.

"Are you all right, love?" the paramedic who was checking Charlie's vital signs asked.

"I'm sorry. She's my only daughter, and I…I'd be lost without her."

"I understand. Talk to her. A mother's voice has healing qualities that people just don't realise. I'm sure she'll pull through this."

Lorne smiled at the young paramedic, who had a kind face and sparkling brown eyes. "I hope so. Thank you."

From there until they reached the hospital, she talked non-stop, reminiscing about the happy times they'd had together throughout her short life. She glanced up at the paramedic now and then to see him smiling and shaking his head at some of the antics they'd got up to together over the years, and that was when it dawned on her that maybe she hadn't been such a terrible mother after all.

Charlie was immediately wheeled through the emergency entrance to a team of medical staff waiting in an Accident and Emergency examination room. Lorne was left pacing the hallway outside, and Katy found her a few minutes later.

"Any news yet?"

"Not yet, Katy. Her pulse and heart rate were steady on the journey over here, which is a good sign."

"I rang Tony, and he told me to send you his love and that he'll get here when he can. He wasn't looking forward to ringing your ex, but agreed to do it."

"I don't envy him that task. Tom is going to blow a gasket."

"Just let him try. I'm sure Tony will point out that Charlie went missing on his watch and not yours," Katy reassured her.

"That's the thing—I really don't want to apportion any blame. We all know what teenagers are like. I'm sure when Charlie eventually comes 'round, she'll be riddled with guilt and apologetic. If only kids would put their brains into gear before getting into bother instead of after. She's been through a lot over the years; I'd have thought that she of all people would know right from wrong by now."

Katy shrugged and sat down in one of the plastic chairs that lined the wall. "Like you said, we all know what teenagers are like. We were teenagers once, remember? Don't tell me you didn't like to push the boundaries now and again; I know I did. Drove my parents 'round the twist on more than one occasion. Once, when I was fourteen, I went missing for a whole weekend."

Lorne lowered herself into the seat next to Katy. "You didn't! Why? Where did you go?"

Katy looked embarrassed. "Umm…a friend and I bought tickets on the internet for Glastonbury."

"Eww…the thought of seeing all those rock bands, cheering them on when you're knee-deep in mud, has never appealed to me. God, I bet your parents were livid when they found out."

"Er, yeah! I was grounded for a whole month, no pocket money, and my chores around the house doubled. I was so knackered by the end of my lockdown that I never did anything like that again."

The swing doors opened beside them and the doctor exited the examination room.

"Mrs. Simpkins?"

"That's right. How is Charlie, Doctor?"

"Hard to say right now, due to the sedation. Her vital signs are nearing normal; however, we won't know the extent of the damage done—if any—until she's fully awake. There could be a possibility of internal bleeding. We're transferring her to the Intensive Care Unit, where she'll be monitored at all times. I suggest you go home and rest. I think she'll be out for a while longer yet."

Lorne's hand clutched at her chest. "I can't leave her."

"That's your choice, but you won't be doing either you or Charlie any favours. I'll tell the ICU sister to contact you the second she wakes up."

"He's right, you know. You should go home and get some rest," Katy agreed, nudging Lorne's elbow.

Lorne dug in her handbag and located one of her business cards. She gave it to the doctor and stood up, ready to leave.

The doctor tucked the card into the top pocket of his white coat. "Please try not to worry. Charlie is in safe hands."

"Thank you, Doctor." Lorne watched him turn and head back into the room, and she mentally kicked herself for not asking to see Charlie one last time before they left. "Let's get out of here."

"I'm driving," Katy insisted.

Lorne nodded, too tired to argue with her. Instead she rang Tony to let him know they were on their way home. Then they made their way out to the car park in silence.

As they drove down one of the country roads a few miles from home, Katy said, "Christ, you certainly get some maniacs on these roads, don't you?"

The inside of the car lit up when the car behind them turned on its main beam. "Indicate and pull over, Katy; let the dickhead pass."

Katy did as Lorne had requested, but instead of overtaking them, the car slowed down and remained close to their rear bumper. The two women looked at each other and frowned.

"If I didn't know any better, I'd say that that was the same car that wrecked Croft's car." No sooner had Lorne uttered the words than the car rammed them from behind. She reached out and helped Katy hold the steering wheel steady. The car behind them revved its engine. They were doing about thirty miles an hour, and Lorne watched their speed increase to over fifty as the four-by-four locked bumpers with the Nova.

"Shit. What do I do?" Katy's panicked voice filled the car.

"Hold her steady. Try braking."

"I am; it's pointless. He's going to fucking kill us!" Katy shrieked.

CHAPTER THIRTEEN

The four-by-four kept ramming them, tentatively at first, but the driver's aggression grew the more Katy fought him off.

"What are we going to do?" Lorne cried out, pictures of her seriously injured child circulating in her mind and hampering her ability to think straight.

"I'm worried about your dad's car, Lorne."

"Sod his car—do what you have to do to save us."

With permission given, Lorne felt the car lurch forward as Katy pressed her foot down hard on the accelerator.

"We'll see what he makes of this. I forgot to tell you that I took an advanced driving course a couple of months back."

If the situation hadn't been so fraught, she would have laughed at Katy's statement, but instead, a feeling of confidence descended over her. However, a huge doubt still persisted as to whether or not they'd make it out of this situation alive.

Lorne grabbed her mobile and dialled 9-9-9. "Yes, it's an emergency. Someone is trying to force us off the road." Suddenly, her brain shifted up a gear and she hung up. "What the hell am I ringing them for?"

Katy shrugged as she focused on pulling away from the charging vehicle.

Lorne dialled another number. "Sean, help us!"

"What the fu—Lorne, is that you? What's going on?"

Lorne heard his chair scrape on the floorboards in his office. "Sean, someone's trying to kill us. Help us, please! We're not far from the house. I really don't want to lead them there. Meet us at Willow Lane by the junction of Mill Road. Get help, quickly."

"I'm on my way. Keep the line free. I'll get back to you soon."

"Thanks, Sean." She hung up and quickly rang home. "Tony, just listen. The same vehicle that attacked us the other night is trying to force us off the road. We're not far away—Willow Lane—but I don't want to lead him back to you. We'll drive past the end of our road."

"I'll get the van—hang on tight. I'll be with you soon. Love you."

Lorne pressed the button to end the call as the Nova received a mighty shove from behind and her mobile shot out of her hand. "Shit, Katy, he's trying to push us into the ditch."

"I'm doing my best, I'm struggling to hold him off. Another shunt like that, and we're gonners."

Within seconds, Katy's prediction came true. The four-by-four rammed them again and kept the pressure on, and Katy stepped on the brakes. The squeal of tyres combined with the whine of the engine deafened them. Another shunt and all of a sudden, the Nova veered off the road and into the narrow ditch. The four-by-four slowed down beside them. With the windows blacked out they couldn't tell what the driver was doing, but they could make an intelligent guess. Lorne gave him the finger, and the driver put his foot down and roared away.

"You okay?" she asked, looking down at Katy, who appeared to be at a steeper angle than she was.

"Yeah, just took a whack in the thigh. You?"

"No, I'm bloody livid." Lorne's mobile rang; they could hear it playing the Sweeney theme tune, but had trouble locating it. "Damn, it's down by my feet somewhere," Katy cried out, frustrated.

"What if you took your seatbelt off?"

Katy unlatched the seatbelt and subsequently fell against the door. "Ouch! Great idea, Lorne, thanks for that." She grappled for the door handle and eased the door open.

"Be careful, hold on to the—" Before Lorne could finish warning her, Katy toppled out of the car and into the ditch, which was half-full of muddy water after the heavy rain that had fallen during the week.

"Crap!" Guided by the interior light, Katy found the phone and handed it to Lorne.

"Hi Sean."

"I'm ten minutes away and a patrol car should be with you soon."

"Don't rush. We're in a ditch. The bastard drove us off the road and disappeared."

"Did you get the plate number?"

"He didn't have one, just like the other night."

"What do you mean, Lorne?"

She could hear the concern in his voice. "It's the same car that crushed Croft's vehicle. It's probably the same guy or guys who put Croft in hospital, too. Don't worry, we're fine."

"Christ, what have you got yourself caught up in this time?"

"Tony's here now. I'll tell you all about it when you get here." She hung up as Tony opened her car door and yanked her free of the car. He held her tight and pressed his lips against her forehead.

"Baby, are you all right?"

Lorne pushed away from him and kissed his lips. "I'm fine. We're fine, aren't we, Katy?"

In the dim light, Lorne saw Katy's head drop to survey the damage to her clothes. She shook out her legs one at a time, which proved pointless as she placed them back in the water after each shake.

Grinning, Tony said, "Climb back through the car, Katy. I'll hoist you out."

Seconds later, Katy was standing alongside them, dripping from her knees down. They heard a distant siren, and soon a police car came to a halt in front of them with its engine ticking. One of the coppers put down his window. "You guys okay?"

"Yeah, we're fine. The car that forced us off the road headed that way. It might be worth taking a look in case the driver is up the road spying on us, monitoring the situation."

"We'll do that. I'll call a breakdown truck to help you."

"Don't bother, I've got a tow bar on the van," Tony said, pointing over his shoulder.

"Righto! We'll be back in a mo'."

They watched the police car turn around and head in the same direction as the four-by-four.

"He'll be miles away by now," Lorne said. "Come on, let's see if we can pull the car out."

"You two stand back—I'll do it. Actually, go sit in the van before you catch a death—especially you, Katy. Hey, don't let me stop you from stripping off those wet clothes."

Katy shook her head and Lorne swiped his arm. "Perv! Are you sure you don't need a hand getting the car out?"

"Nope."

Lorne and Katy got in the back of the van and watched Tony attach the towrope between the Nova and the van. They had to stifle a laugh when he jumped down into the ditch and forgot it was half-full of filthy water.

Another car pulled up and Sean got out. He shook hands with Tony and went over to see if he could help. Between them, they managed to get the Nova back on the road. Surprisingly, it started on the first try. Katy and Lorne left the van to survey the damage at the rear. The car was a mess. The bumper was hanging off at one end and dragging on the ground. Tony gave it a good yank, and without too much effort the bumper came completely away from the car.

"Built to last, obviously," Sean joked. "Can we go back to your place and have a chat?"

"That'd be good. Katy and I will take the Nova."

Lorne jumped in the driver's seat and Katy held her wet trousers away from her skin in the passenger's seat beside her. It took them five minutes to get back to the house. Lorne's father, his face twisted in anxiety, came to meet them in the drive.

"We're fine, Dad. Charlie's in a coma, the doctor insisted we should come home. Sorry about the car; I'll get it repaired for you."

"If you had been back at the hospital this wouldn't have happened. Poor Charlie, are you going back there?" her father said abruptly.

Lorne frowned it wasn't like her father to be so abrupt with her. "Are you sure you're all right, Dad?"

He waved a hand at her. "I'm fine, concerned about everyone as usual. About Charlie and you girls, of course. Sean, it's good to see you again." Sam shook Sean's hand.

Lorne knew not to push things with her father. The group walked into the house. Katy went upstairs to her room to change her clothes and joined in the conversation upon her return.

Sean turned to Katy, his brow furrowed. "So you've been working on this case at the station?"

Katy swallowed and looked guilty. "Yeah, but only a little."

"What do you mean by that?"

"I mean, I kept coming up against a wall. Something stinks. I told Lorne my suspicions and she said it resembled what happened when Charlie was abducted. Certain doors closed during that case, as well." Katy glanced over at Lorne for backup.

"We all know what we're dealing with here, Sean. People with money, not knowing what to spend it on, going down the perverted sex route. Men out to fulfill their petty little sexual fantasies. Croft has stumbled upon a massive import business, and I'm going to do everything in my power to put a stop to the business before it gets out of control. Innocent people are either dying or being sold into slavery, and for what? The promise of a far better life, that's what.

I've rid the world of one of these bastards already; if I have to spend the rest of my life hunting these sick shits down, I'll do it."

Tony sought her hand. "We'll do it."

Then Katy grabbed Lorne's other hand. "Yes, we'll do it. Hey, we could be the Three Musketeers, I want to be D'Artagnan."

Sean cleared his throat. "DS Foster, you're forgetting one thing."

"I am?" Katy said, her tone riddled with sarcasm.

"You're still employed by the Met," Sean stated, raising an eyebrow.

Lorne snorted. "Well, it's a shame the Met doesn't value her as much as we do. Answer me one thing, Sean: would a male officer have been put in Katy's position? No, they wouldn't. Over the years, I've witnessed plenty of incidents where a male officer has hit a prisoner or suspect. Christ, Pete even did it a few times, and not *once* was he ever suspended or pulled over the coals for it."

"The Met has changed, Lorne. Prisoners are touting the human rights card nowadays."

"That's bullshit and you bloody know it. Sort it out, Sean, or Katy will join our team. Won't you, Katy?"

"Damn right. I like to feel appreciated at work, and to be honest, I know Lorne had her problems when she worked for the Met, and, well, I can see the same thing happening to me. A person can only take so much of being unappreciated—surely you can see that, sir."

He held his hands up. "Hey, you don't have to convince me, Katy. Lorne will tell you that I was on her side at all times."

Lorne narrowed her eyes at him. "Hmm…a touch of selective memory there, I think, Sean. Anyway, do what you can for her. The Met still has major problems with equality. If this isn't resolved soon, I've advised Katy to bypass the union rep and employ a good solicitor." She placed a hand on either side of her head and said, "I can foresee plenty of compensation coming your way, young lady, and in the not too distant future."

Lorne's antics broke the ice a little and they all laughed—everyone except her father. "Everything all right, Dad? You seem a little distant this evening."

"Apart from nearly losing my daughter and my granddaughter, yep, everything is just dandy."

"Sorry, Dad, that was insensitive of me. The doctor assured me the hospital would ring the minute she wakes up."

"Well, I'm not sure you should be involved in this case. Yes, you have Katy and Sean to fall back on in the Force, but with our limited resources, I don't see what you can do to stop this gang, Lorne."

"Neither do I, yet. But I have to try. Don't forget that Tony has excellent contacts, as well. Everything is all a bit thin on the ground at the moment. Maybe that'll change when Katy and I visit the agency on Monday."

"Agency? What agency?" Sean interrupted.

Lorne went through what they had uncovered about the case so far. The two wealthy homes she had visited whose maids/au pairs had each lost family members in the shipwreck. "We rang the agency to get their side of the story the other day, and they were more than a little evasive with their answers. I think a face-to-face visit might remedy that. We've tried to research the agency, but keep coming up blank. Sounds to me like it's a front for something more sinister."

"Human trafficking, you mean?" Sean asked, looking thoughtful.

"Human trafficking, prostitution, I wouldn't put it past them to be involved with the latest craze to hit our shores snuff movies either—all the heinous crimes you can think of to do with the sex trade, I bet you'll find a connection at that agency."

"The owner is hardly going to admit to anything when you arrive on her doorstep, Lorne."

"Yeah, I know that, thanks for pointing it out, Sean, but *I have ways of making people talk*," she said in her best Herr Flick voice.

The doorbell rang, and Tony opened the back door. He paid the bloke in the crash helmet thirty pounds and took the two brown take-away bags from him. Lorne left the table and went over to the oven to collect the warmed plates and proceeded to dish up the Indian meal. "Bit of everything for all of you?"

They all agreed and hungrily queued up to take a plate once Lorne had finished serving up.

Sean left a little after ten o'clock and they all decided to turn in for the night after their exhausting day. Lorne quickly rang the ICU to ask if Charlie's condition had changed, but it hadn't. The night sister reassured her that if Charlie regained consciousness, she would ring Lorne immediately, day or night. Safe in the knowledge that her daughter was being well cared for by experienced medical staff, Lorne went to bed, she slept fitfully that night, and even had a nightmare in which she had been driven off the road and ended up in a river, fighting for breath.

CHAPTER FOURTEEN

The telephone woke them at ten past seven the next morning. Lorne sat upright in bed and answered it on the second ring. "Hello?"

"Mrs. Simpkins, it's the ICU. We're pleased to inform you that Charlie has now woken up. You're free to visit at any time."

"Is she talking? Is she moving? Is she in pain?" She fired the questions off one after the other without pausing long enough for the nurse to answer.

"Yes, she's talking, and yes, she's in pain. We'll have a chat when you get here."

"Oh, thank you so much. Tell her I'll be with her within the hour."

"I will. Please drive safely, there's no need to rush."

Lorne replaced the phone on the bedside table and enthusiastically shook her husband. "Tony, Tony—she's awake."

"That's great, hon. Do you want me to come with you?"

"Someone has to stay here and look after this place, I'm not sure dad is up to it at the moment, he looked exhausted to me yesterday."

He sat up. "You get ready; I'll stay here and see to the dogs. Take Katy with you—oh, and you'd better ring Tom before you go."

She turned and kissed him hard on the cheek. "I'll ring him after I've had a shower." She leapt out of the bed and skipped into the bathroom, where she found herself singing one of Charlie's favourite songs during her shower. *"Don't ya wish your girlfriend was hot like me? Don't ya, don't ya..."*

Before getting dressed, she walked along the hallway to Charlie's room, where Katy was sleeping, and tapped on the door. "Katy, are you awake?"

"I am now," came Katy's muffled reply.

"Get dressed, hon, we have to get to the hospital. Charlie's awake."

Lorne heard the bed springs boing and Katy groaned as if one of the springs had dug in her as she moved. "That's wonderful news. Can I grab a quick shower?"

"Of course. I'll knock up some breakfast."

"I don't want any of that leftover curry—my stomach is too delicate this morning."

Lorne laughed. "I'll fix you some toast and marmalade. We don't do leftovers in this house."

She ran back into the bedroom, threw on a pair of jeans and a fleecy jumper to ward off the chill of the morning, and went downstairs. Henry was at the kitchen door, whining to go out. "Sorry, pal, I guess in all the excitement I forgot about you." She hugged him and kissed his nose. "Charlie's coming home." Henry reached out a paw and scratched the back door. "All right, matey, there you go." She opened the door and watched him run over to the large hydrangea bush near the entrance of the drive and cock his leg.

She had to wait for her guest to stop running the shower before she could fill the kettle. Katy came downstairs approximately ten minutes later. Lorne placed a cup of coffee and two slices of toast in front of Katy, and then took a cup of coffee in to her father. By now, it was almost seven thirty.

Her father stirred as she entered his room. "I heard the phone. Was it the hospital, love?"

"Good news, Dad," she said, noting how pale he looked. "Charlie's awake. Katy and I are just going to leave now. The sister said she's in pain; I don't know how much, though. I'll find out more when I get there. Damn, we forgot to ring Jade last night to tell her."

Her father moaned as he sat up in bed, and Lorne pulled the pillow up behind him to ensure that he was comfortable. "Leave Jade to me. You just be concerned about your daughter. Let's hope she's going to be okay—for all our sakes."

"Meaning what, exactly, Dad?"

"This place, for instance. To be honest, love, I'm not sure I can help out much more. Everything is so much effort these days."

Lorne was aghast; it was the first time he'd confided in her that he was struggling to cope. Had she really been taking him for granted that much? That was another thing she'd have to sort out sooner rather than later. If Katy came on board with the P.I. business, that would leave her more time to care for the animals—it was her responsibility, after all, and no one else's. Guilt wrapped around her like a cold mist. Where would she be without her family to fall back on? Was she expecting too much of them? If they were finding it hard, wouldn't they let her know?

"Lorne?" Her father rested his hand on her face.

"Sorry, Dad, I was just thinking. I've put too much on your shoulders—please forgive me."

"Stop it! There's nothing to forgive. Maybe that meningitis a few months back took more out of me than I first thought."

"Do you want me to ring the doctor?"

She knew what his answer would be before he said it.

"Nope."

"Okay. Bear with me a couple of days. I'll try and sort things out this week, Dad, I promise."

"Shoo—go now. Give Charlie a kiss for me and tell her I love her."

Lorne bent down and pecked him on the cheek. "I will, Dad. Stay in bed for a while. Tony said he'll take care of the dogs this morning."

"Maybe I will have a bit of a lie in, love," he replied, his voice as weary as his smile.

Lorne closed the door to her father's room gently behind her and made her way back in to the kitchen, where Katy was waiting for her.

"Hey, why the sad face? You should be happy Charlie is awake."

"I am, Katy. It's Dad I'm worried about. You saw how quiet he was while we were eating last night. That's unheard of when we're discussing a case. I just took a coffee to him and he looks spent, totally worn out. Maybe I better rethink the two businesses and my family's parts in them. I'm not sure what's going to happen with Charlie yet," she said, concerned she reached for the jacket that she had hooked over the kitchen chair and put it on.

"I'm sure Charlie will be fine once she's home safe, and well. I'm guessing your dad will be fine too, once his granddaughter is out of hospital. Keep positive, girl." Katy smiled and gave Lorne's arm a reassuring rub.

"Damn!" She cuddled Katy. "Happy birthday, sweetie." Lorne released Katy, whose cheeks had turned a fetching crimson.

"Some birthday. I'm not likely to forget this one in a hurry, am I?"

"Sorry, hon."

Katy raised a hand. "Enough already. Let's go see how that daughter of yours is."

* * *

They walked into the ICU to see Charlie crying as she spoke to a doctor. Lorne rushed to her bedside. Gripping Charlie's shaking hand in hers, she asked the doctor, "What's going on?"

Katy stood back, but Lorne beckoned her friend to come forward. By the serious expression on the doctor's face, she was going to need all the support she could get.

"Mrs. Simpkins, I take it?" the young male doctor asked. His tone was offhand and as far away from caring as she could imagine.

"That's right. I said: what's going on? Why is my daughter crying?" Her tone matched his.

Between sobs, Charlie spoke instead of the doctor. "Mum, I can't feel my legs and they won't tell me how Simon is."

They were the worst words she could have imagined hearing. Her beautiful daughter was paralysed because she'd been foolishly coaxed into a boy's car. Lorne forced the tears back, adamant that she should stay strong for Charlie's sake. The Simon issue would have to be dealt with later. She brushed the hair out of her daughter's eyes and delved into her pocket for a tissue to wipe away the tears that were coursing down Charlie's pale cheeks. "Hush, baby. I'm going to talk to the doctor alone. Look, Katy's come to see you." Lorne glanced over her shoulder at Katy and gave her a pleading look.

The doctor tutted and turned away from the bed. Lorne followed him, her legs trembling beneath her.

"What's the meaning of this? How dare you tell her something like that!"

"Now, wait just a minute. I walked on the ward a few seconds before you arrived. I told your daughter nothing."

His whole body appeared to stiffen in front of her. She was conscious of Charlie's sharp hearing and lowered her voice. "Then why would she say such a thing?" Lorne asked, confused.

"Maybe because it's a fact—she *can't* feel her legs. It sometimes happens after a bad crash. However, that does not mean it's permanent. She could regain the feeling soon; the nerves could spark into life at any moment, or there could be a delay of a week or so. We'll need to carry out further tests to be sure." His face cracked into a forced smile and his voice appeared to have softened a little. So much so that Lorne felt the need to apologise for her behaviour.

"I'm sorry, I misconstrued the situation. I suppose it was a gut reaction to think she could be paralysed. What percentages are we talking about here?"

"I'd say your daughter has a fifty to eighty percent chance of walking again, but the tests will tell us more. Let's see what the results say and then we'll be more certain about our facts. Sit with her for a while. I'll see if we can find the staff I need to carry out the relevant tests; on Sundays, the staffing level is lower than during the week."

Lorne nodded and turned to see Katy and Charlie watching them. She smiled at her daughter and blew her a kiss. "Thank you. Is there anything we can do for Charlie in the meantime?"

"No. Just comfort her, try to take her mind off her injuries. It won't be easy, I know, but it'll help her recover. I'll be back soon." He exited the ward and Lorne returned to sit on the edge of her daughter's bed.

"Well? What did he say? Will I have to spend the rest of my life in a wheelchair?" Charlie asked as fresh tears fell from her eyes.

"They have to run some tests, darling. Hey, I had a word with the doc, told him we need you mucking out kennels before the end of next week. I'll tell you what—I'll make a deal with you: I won't clean the kennels out all week. That'll keep you busy for a couple of hours next weekend, won't it?"

Charlie cringed at the thought but a smile settled on her face. "Eww...at the rate those guys poop, I'll have a pile the size of Everest to contend with."

Lorne laughed. "You haven't met the new recruits yet—a Great Dane and an Irish Wolfhound—now those guys can poop for England." She pulled a face and held her nose for a second. "And the smell..."

The three of them laughed and chatted non-stop about girly things for the next fifteen minutes or so until the doctor returned. He motioned with his head for Lorne to join him near the sister's desk at the end of the ward.

"Tests will begin in an hour. We'll have a clearer indication of what we're dealing with then."

"Thank you, Doctor. I'm sorry about what happened before."

"Don't worry. Dealing with irate parents goes with the job."

Lorne found herself smiling, despite the mild insult. "Will Charlie be awake during the tests?"

"Of course—they are primarily to measure the amount of pain your daughter is in. I'd like you to be there to comfort her, if that's all right."

"I wouldn't have it any other way."

The doctor gave a brief nod. "We'll come and collect her when we're ready."

Lorne went back to let Charlie and Katy know what was going to happen next.

"Well, while that's going on, I'll go and visit Croft," Katy said.

"Makes sense. He'll probably be more lucid today. You might even get a description of the men who beat him up."

"Hey, what's this?" Charlie piped up, her mood seemed a little brighter after their girly chat.

Lorne tapped the end of Charlie's nose and winked at her. "Never you mind, Miss Nosey Parker. Your number one priority is getting yourself better."

Charlie eyed her suspiciously and murmured, "What, no major telling off for being stupid?"

"Were you stupid, Charlie?"

Her daughter's head slipped round to face the wall. "Yes. I didn't mean it. Simon wanted to show me the car his father had bought."

Katy stood up to leave. "I can sense a heavy mother-daughter talk coming on. See you in an hour or so."

After Katy left, Lorne sat on the edge of her daughter's bed and put a finger under Charlie's chin, forcing her daughter to look her in the eye. "We've talked about this, haven't we, Charlie?"

"I know I've let you down, Mum, but Simon said it would be a quick spin around the block...I tried to make him stop. He kept laughing at me, calling me a wuss. In the end, I tugged on his arm to try and force him to take me home and...and that's when it happened. Why did I mess around while he was driving? Why? Now this!" She pointed down at her legs.

"Hush now. What's done is done. You're alive. That's the main thing."

Charlie narrowed her eyes. "Meaning? No! Simon's not..."

"I'm sorry, sweetheart, but Simon didn't make it."

Charlie buried her face in her trembling hands and sobbed. Lorne ran a hand over Charlie's head, and a small lump formed in her throat.

The awkward silence between them was disturbed by footsteps approaching on the tiled floor. Lorne glanced up at the doctor, who was observing them with a look of concern. Lorne shook her head, silently telling him not to worry.

"We're ready for you now, Charlie."

* * *

Katy knocked on Croft's door and walked into the room.

The injured man stirred and opened a bruised eye to look at her. He seemed briefly scared by her entrance, but then recognition registered on his face and he visibly relaxed and motioned for her to sit beside him.

"How are you feeling?"

"Sore." He sat up and grimaced.

"I'm sorry this happened to you. Will you take heed of the warning now?" Katy asked, lowering herself into the wooden chair next to his bed.

"If you think that, you don't know me."

Katy sighed. "These are very serious people you're dealing with, Croft."

"Have you come here to reprimand me, or would you like me to share the new information I've just received?" A teasing look manifested in his eyes.

Katy sat forward and teetered on the edge of the seat. "Information? What information?"

"The information I received about half an hour ago from one of my informants," Croft said with a smirk that he quickly seemed to regret.

Katy snapped into detective mode, delving into her pocket and pulling out her pad and a pen. "About the traffickers, I take it?"

"That's right."

"Well, come on. Don't draw it out," Katy said impatiently.

"There's talk on the streets that another delivery is due."

"Due? When?" Katy asked, her pen poised ready to jot down the details. Her heart started to race at the thought of finally bringing this gang down.

"Look at you. Your heart's pumping like an express train, isn't it? If we swapped places, you wouldn't be able to give this case up, either, would you?"

"Where?" she demanded, ignoring his comment.

"Same place—the warehouse out on the trading estate."

"When? God, are you always such a pain in the arse?" Katy doodled on the pad as a way of venting her frustration.

"I have my moments."

"Croft, you would try the patience of a saint. When?"

"Okay, you win. Tonight, at nine o'clock."

"This source of yours—is he kosher? Guaranteed tip off, is it?"

"Give or take on the time; it's a guesstimate. Depends on the authorities, etc. But yes, you can take my word that this is a guaranteed tip off."

"Anything else?" Katy asked, her mind already forming the foundation of a plan.

Surprised, he asked, "Isn't that enough? In the future remind me to tell my informants that they must do better for this pretty detective I know."

Katy refused to blush, used to dealing with jerks like him, she shook her head and gave him one of her 'you sad bastard' looks.

He got the hint and gave her a cheeky wink as she stood up to leave. "We'll let you know what happens." Katy waved her notebook at him before tucking it back into her jacket pocket. "Thanks for the tipoff."

"Let's hope something comes of it, for the girls' sake. Be careful out there," she heard him say as she closed the door behind her.

Lost in thought, she made her way through the long, narrow corridors back to the ICU, completely unaware that someone was following her.

CHAPTER FIFTEEN

Lorne settled her daughter into bed, consciously holding back her own tears. For poor Charlie the dam had broken; she was sobbing and gasping for air between sobs when Katy returned to the ward.

"Can you stay with Charlie for a minute, Katy? I need to have another chat with the doctor."

"Of course." Katy sat on the edge of the bed and held Charlie's trembling hand, squeezing it between hers.

As Lorne walked over to the sister's desk she heard Katy asking Charlie about the latest music groups she liked. She felt relieved when Charlie's crying stopped and her daughter responded enthusiastically.

The doctor was looking at the test results when Lorne joined him. "Well?"

"It doesn't look good, I'm afraid. Charlie appears to have no feeling in her legs at all. Whether that will change over the coming weeks, we have no idea. The X-rays didn't really show us anything, either."

"Could it be a trapped nerve?" Lorne asked more out of hope than anything else.

"It could be. I'm sorry, but it's going to be a waiting game over the next few weeks. A physiotherapist will get to work on Charlie tomorrow. It's surprising what results can be obtained from manipulating the muscles, joints, and limbs."

"I see," she mumbled, downhearted by the news.

"Don't give up—we won't. Is her father around?" the doctor asked with a slight smile.

"We're divorced. Actually, Charlie lives with him."

"In my experience, the burden of keeping her spirits up shouldn't be down to one person. Can you take it in turns to visit? I wouldn't advise being here all the time; she should have different people around her—it'll aid in her recovery in the long run."

Lorne cringed at the thought of asking Tom to share in the role of visiting and encouraging Charlie. It was going to be a tough enough task for her, let alone him. He wasn't blessed with an abundance of patience, and he was in the process of expanding his mechanics business after buying a second garage. She knew his time at present was limited. *But hey, so is mine. If I can visit our one and only child, then I'm sure he can do his share, too.*

"I'll have a word with him. I'm sure we can come up with some kind of workable schedule."

"Excellent. If you ever need to chat, the sister or her staff can page me. I'm always around—during the day, at least."

"Thank you. I'll call Tom—her father—straight away."

Lorne had a brief chat with Charlie and Katy, then drew in a deep breath and wandered outside the unit to locate a public telephone.

When Tom answered, thankfully, she informed him of their daughter's prognosis without the usual interruptions; in fact, he was at a loss for words once she had finished running through everything the doctor had told her.

"Tom, are you still there?" she asked quietly.

He snuffled and then replied, "I'm here. Shit, Lorne, what are we going to do?"

"Be there for her. I won't be able to do this alone, Tom."

"I wouldn't expect you to. What kind of person do you take me for?" he snapped.

"I'm sorry. I know you're very busy; I am too, do you think we can work something out for Charlie's sake?"

"Of course. I can come down and spend the day with her today, if it'll help."

Relief filled her. "That'd be great, Tom. How long will you be?"

"I'll be there in an hour. We'll have a chat then."

For the next hour, Lorne and Katy did an excellent job of keeping Charlie's mind off her injuries. Charlie insisted they tell her about some of the cases they had worked on in the past. Lorne was careful not to divulge too much about the more gruesome cases she'd worked on, and Katy took her lead to do the same. Approximately an hour later, Tom walked through the doors to the ICU. He looked as if he hadn't slept or shaved for weeks. Lorne felt guilty for calling him, but then he had a right to know what was going on with Charlie, and it had been his decision to come to the hospital to be with his daughter, not hers.

Lorne and Katy left approximately thirty minutes later. Charlie seemed happy to be left alone with her dad. "I'll call you this afternoon," Lorne told her daughter before leaving.

Once they were settled in the car and on the way home, Katy said, "You haven't asked how things went with Croft."

Lorne glanced sideways as she navigated the bollards at road works in the road. "Umm...I've been a little preoccupied, in case you hadn't noticed."

"Yeah, sorry. I've been dying to tell you. He's had contact with his informant."

"What? In the hospital?"

Katy shrugged. "Maybe they rang up pretending to be a family member."

"Perhaps. Go on."

"There's another delivery due tonight."

"Shit! Where?"

"Apparently the same place as before, around nine o'clock, give or take," Katy told her.

Lorne was quiet for a few seconds as things slotted into place in her mind. "If I get Tom to stay with Charlie for the rest of the day, we could go down there this evening."

"*We*? Meaning who?"

"You, me, and Tony. I don't think it would be wise for us two going down there alone, do you?"

Katy shook her head vigorously. "Not after what happened to Croft, no. Will Tony be up for it?"

"You bet. He wants this stopped as much as we do, even more so since that four-by-four drove us off the road. That reminds me, I must sort dad's car out—I'm not sure I can drive around in the van much longer." She tapped the steering wheel with her fist. "I should've asked Tom if he would repair it."

"I wouldn't, if I were in your shoes."

Puzzled, Lorne asked, "Why?"

"It might highlight how dangerous the P.I. business can be, and he might think twice about letting Charlie stay with you at the weekends."

"Good point. It's not been much of a birthday for you so far, has it?"

"Will you stop it! I'm having the time of my life."

Lorne laughed and shook her head. "I promise I'll make it up to you."

"Nonsense. Really, I wouldn't have it any other way."

* * *

Tension hung heavy in the air as darkness fell around them like an ominous warning.

Between them, they had agreed that Tony should take charge of the covert operation—he was the expert, after all. At the scene, he coordinated their positions with few words and plenty of pointing. Once or twice, Lorne and Katy glanced at each other with a look that said 'he's in his element, we better do as we're told or else.'

By the time the lorry pulled up at the yard, they had been in position for a full fifteen minutes. Two men opened the large gates while the driver steered the vehicle through the opening. The gates shut behind the lorry and then Lorne, Katy, and Tony moved into their second allocated positions. Tony had sourced good viewing spots for them all. Once the gates were opened again, they would have to sprint back to their original positions before the gang spotted them. From this angle, they could observe what was happening and would be able to decide when to make the appropriate move back to safety.

Lorne crouched down by a spy hole in the tin fence. She saw the three men move to the rear of the lorry, laughing and sharing dirty jokes as they unlatched the back of the truck. Her heart rate escalated when she heard the frightened squeals of several young women. Straining, she could faintly hear what sounded like frightened jabbering in a language that sounded Asian. She heard some form of scraping on the floor of the lorry, as if containers or boxes were being moved, then one of the men shouted at whoever was inside to "get a move on."

Katy waved to get Lorne's attention. "Can you see anything?" Katy mouthed.

"Not a lot. You?" Lorne mouthed back.

Katy shook her head in frustration. Lorne held a finger up, telling Katy to wait a moment as she watched a line of girls leave the lorry and walk towards the huge warehouse. She counted until the last person was shoved through the door and it slammed shut behind them. Twenty-five scared, frantic young girls, clinging to each other as if their lives depended on it, disappeared into the warehouse and out of sight. Lorne looked over at Tony, his face set like stone. He held a hand up, ordering her to remain in place. She wanted to dive in and rescue the girls when the men punched each other in the arm before they entered the warehouse. The gesture sickened her; it wasn't difficult to understand what their deviant intentions were.

The second the warehouse door shut, Tony made his move. He did his best; however, his prosthetic leg hampered his ability to run in a crouched position. There was a window to the right of the door just in front of where Lorne and Katy were positioned. With his back pressed against the wall, Tony slowly craned his neck to look inside the warehouse.

Lorne was on tenterhooks. What if the men changed their minds and came barging out of there and caught him? What then? Without realising she had done it, she crossed her fingers on both hands.

"Hey! Don't worry—he'll be fine," Katy called over in a hushed voice.

"It's natural, I'm a born worrier," she replied, not taking her eyes off her husband.

Tony ducked under the window and positioned himself on the other side. Lorne suspected it was to gain a better view. She saw him wince on more than one occasion, and looked down at his hands, his fists were continually clenching open and shut.

She saw Tony wave a hand, motioning Katy and her to duck just before one of the overweight men threw open the warehouse door. The man zipped up the fly on his jeans and took a packet of cigarettes from his pocket. Lighting one up, he leaned back against the door and blew out a satisfied smoke ring.

You sick bastard! If that is the only way you can get your fucking kicks. Lorne shook her head in disgust before the seriousness of the situation hit home. Tony was about five feet from the guy; one tiny movement could alert him, and that would be game over. Another couple of puffs, and fatman disappeared inside again. Lorne frantically urged Tony to get out of there before another of the criminals came outside for a fag.

Tony rejoined them. "We'd better move back before they shift the truck out."

"What's going on?" Katy naïvely asked.

Neither of them filled her in until they were safely back in the van. "Katy, I can't believe you'd ask such a thing. What do you think those guys were doing in there?" Even in the dim interior light, Lorne could see a tinge of colour seeping into Katy's embarrassed face.

"Sorry, I didn't make myself very clear. It doesn't take much imagination to know what was going on in there. What I should have said was, 'could you make out anything else?' The layout of the warehouse, for instance. Whether the girls were kept there for long, or shipped out immediately," Katy said, giving Lorne the evil eye.

Tony let out an exasperated breath. "At the back of the warehouse, I could just make out some form of…cage, I suppose, for want of a better word. It looked like there were some very thin mattresses in the cage, but I couldn't be certain."

"How could they keep the girls here, even for a day or two? Maybe we should make a call to the council, see what they have to say about this, I'm sure they aren't aware of what's going on here." Lorne said, although she had a feeling that getting in touch with the authorities would alter nothing. She sensed that a few backhanders were possibly flying around, it wouldn't be the first time, as Lorne was all too aware.

Tony shrugged. "It's worth a try, but I sense it will be a pointless exercise. You wouldn't treat animals like that." Tony thumbed behind him. "All right, I didn't expect these girls to be treated like princesses; still, at the moment, after travelling for probably two to three weeks, they're lined up, and those three guys are screwing them every which way."

"Please stop! Tony, I don't want to know," Lorne said, pushing down the bile burning her throat.

The van remained silent all the way back to the house, each of them lost in their own individual thoughts.

* * *

When they got back, they found Lorne's father sitting at the table with Jade, who seemed worried about something.

Lorne gave her a quick hug and introduced Katy to her. "I remember Katy from your wedding. Hi, nice to see you again."

"Likewise," Katy said before she left the room.

"What's up, Jade?" Lorne asked. She switched the kettle on then bent down to have a cuddle with her dog. A cuddle with Henry *always* put life back into perspective.

"Apart from being concerned about Dad? I wanted to see how you got on at Angie's the other day."

Lorne noticed sadness in her sister's eyes. She stood up and made the five of them a drink. "Didn't I ring you the day I visited her?" She wracked her brain. "I'm sure I did."

Irritated, Jade flung her arms in the air. "All right, you rang me."

Lorne walked over to the table and placed a mug of coffee in front of her father and Jade, then returned to fetch Tony's and her own. She sat in the chair next to her sister and gave her a puzzled look. "Let's have it."

Jade inhaled deeply and then released a heavy breath. "It's Angie." She looked down at the table and started turning her mug in her hand.

"Jade, honey, has something happened to her?" The words were hard to get out as Lorne fought the unwanted images rifling through her head. She knew the type of people she was dealing with by now, and anyone who spoke out against them in any way usually found themselves on the wrong end of a beating.

Tears erupted in Jade's eyes and tumbled down her pale cheeks. "I called her and she didn't really want to talk to me. She cut the conversation short, which is unusual for Angie. So I jumped in my car and went over to see her. The butler tried his hardest to prevent me from seeing her, but I shoved past him. Lorne, she was in an absolutely terrible state. She was sitting in her chair—unable to stand, I'm guessing…" Her voice trailed off.

"Why? Why couldn't she stand up, Jade?"

"She was in dreadful pain—she must have been."

Typical Jade, going around the houses as usual instead of getting directly to the point. Lorne prompted her gently. "Jade, can you describe what was wrong with her?"

"Not in a month of Sundays. Covered in bruises, from what I could see. She wore winter clothes, most unusual for Angie. You know, a polo neck and trousers. This time of year, with the weather warming up, she should be wearing her summer clothes."

"Did you ask her what happened?"

"Of course, I did. What do you take me for?"

"All right, Jade, there's no need to snap. I'm only trying to find out what went on."

Their father interjected, "Jade, just tell Lorne what was said." He sounded tired, and having a go at Jade was totally out of character for him.

Jade bristled and grudgingly gave the information. "I asked her what happened and she told me she'd been in a car accident. I know she was lying, though, because I walked past her car in the drive and there wasn't a scratch on it."

"Could she have been driving her husband's car, perhaps?" Lorne asked, perplexed.

"I asked her that; she definitely said it was her car involved in the accident."

"Did you ask if she'd been to hospital?" Tony asked his brow furrowed as he sipped at his coffee.

"I asked, she said she hadn't. That's what I thought was strange. Well, that, and her car not being damaged. Then..." Jade paused for dramatic effect until Lorne urged her to continue.

"Yes?"

"Then, her maid brought us a pot of coffee, and she had bruises, too."

"Jai San?" Lorne asked incredulously.

"What's going on?" Katy asked as she retrieved her coffee off the worktop and joined them at the table.

Lorne filled her in quickly before Jade responded, "If anything, the maid or au pair—whatever she's called—was in a worse state than Angie."

"Shit. We have to do something." Lorne's hand crashed down on the table and her coffee sloshed out of the cup.

"Lorne, we can't. Not yet." Tony looked at her father for support.

"Tony's right. It would be foolish to intervene now."

"What do you suggest then, Dad?" Lorne asked.

"Let's consider your options. You could go down the police route, which so far has drawn a massive blank. You could stick with Croft and his informants—it seems to be bringing some results, though tiny results, admittedly. Nonetheless, it's still delivering possibilities we should be able to work with eventually. Or you could go to the source of the problem. In my opinion, that's the agency. Go and throw your weight around down there."

"You're right! Actually, that was going to be our next stop, wasn't it, Katy?"

Katy gave an assertive nod. "Definitely our number one stop."

"That's settled, then. Katy and I will go to the agency. Tony, can you drop an anonymous call to the council about the warehouse first thing?"

"Yep, already on my extensive to-do list. I'm going to get in touch with MI5, too, see what I can dig up."

"Hang on," Jade said, "What warehouse?"

Not wishing to upset her sister any more than was necessary, Lorne made up something. "Oh, it's another case we're working on." She winked at Tony and her father to back her up.

"That's right, a drugs case. The business is really picking up," her father said with a smile.

"Hey, if ever you need a hand with the kennel side of things—you know, until Charlie gets better—I can help out for a couple of hours during the week. My God, I forgot to ask—how is Charlie?"

Lorne left the others to explain about Charlie while she rang the hospital and spoke to Tom.

CHAPTER SIXTEEN

Lorne and Katy set off before it was light the next morning.

"Are you sure Tony didn't mind doing the chores this morning? He looked pissed off to me," Katy asked with a grin.

Lorne stifled a yawn. It had been a long, sleepless night for her, as she'd been unable to shut out the images of the girls in jeopardy. "He doesn't mind. He probably didn't get much sleep last night. I kept him awake for most of the night."

Katy coughed slightly. "Umm…too much information. You'll be making me blush soon."

"Idiot! Not like that. I just couldn't prevent this case from playing out in my mind. All the old memories came flooding back, which then led me to feel guilty about Charlie and her latest disastrous escapade. Why does life have to be so cruel?"

"Life is always hard. It's how we deal with the scenarios it throws up that counts. Charlie knows that you love her. She'll pull through this latest scrape, I'm sure. She has her mother's determined genes."

Lorne indicated and turned in to the next road on the right. Even in the dark, the area looked dog rough. At the top of the road were several flickering lights. Lorne strained to make out what they were and gasped when she realised it was a tiny community—a cardboard city settlement. She shuddered at the thought of people living on the streets.

After locating the correct address, Lorne parked the car in a space a few doors down from the agency. They waited for the sun to come up and Tara Small to arrive.

"How are we going to handle this?" Katy asked, resting her head back against the headrest of her seat.

"Not entirely sure yet. Let's see what we pick up, and we'll go from there. Do you think halfway through the conversation you could ask to use the loo and take a snoop around?"

"Sure thing. I bet she doesn't allow it, though, I can feel that in my water."

They both chuckled. They had to wait for over an hour until they noted the first flurry of activity at the address. Two skinny girls left the building. They staggered down the steps, their arms tightly linked.

"Are they drunk? What are they doing coming *out* of the building? I expected to see people turning up here, not leaving," Lorne said.

Katy pointed as the door to the property opened just wide enough to let another two people out. This time, two men emerged. "Wait, there's more."

"Interesting." Lorne craned her neck to look up at the three-storey building. "Could this be some form of bedsit property, do you think? Or could these girls be using this property as some kind of brothel?"

"It's hard to tell. If it is a brothel, would they be letting these girls go off on their own? Are those two men customers or what?" Katy joined in.

"That seems to be the end of people leaving, although I can see a few lights on at the very top of the house."

Katy leaned forward in her seat. "Yeah, I can see, in the attic. That sounds more like it: make the girls live in a tiny attic and service men regularly."

"Looks like Tony will be making another anonymous call to the council when we get back. Hang on, this looks like the woman we're after."

A thin black woman got out of a sleek Mercedes AMC sports car and crossed the road to the house. She ran up the dozen or so steps daintily in her six-inch heels. Somehow, Lorne had imagined a rough looking woman with a face like a bulldog, but this woman was the total opposite, if she were indeed Tara Small. There was only one way to find out.

"We'll give her five minutes to get settled in and then surprise her."

Before they could get out of the car, a huge black limo double-parked outside the property and a tall, well-dressed gentleman exited the rear door, walked up the steps, and entered the building.

"Interesting development," Lorne stated, placing her elbows on the steering wheel and resting her chin on her fists. "Wonder what part he plays in all this?"

"You say that as if you know him."

Lorne turned and winked at Katy. "Might, might not."

"You know what? Sometimes you infuriate the hell out of me," Katy retorted with a mock snarl.

"That's why you love working with me. Pete loved it, too; it used to keep him on his chubby toes." She smiled as she remembered her overweight partner, but her smile waned when the gentleman caller returned to his car. "Well, that was short and sweet. We'll go in as soon as the car drives off."

Katy already had her hand on the door handle, eager to leave. The limo eased away gracefully and glided around the corner at the top of the road.

"Let's go."

The early morning sun warmed their faces as they made their way from the car to the house. Lorne tried the handle, and, thankfully, the door opened. The last thing she wanted to do was to announce their arrival and allow whoever was inside to hide any evidence of illegal activity.

In the hallway, there were two doors, one on either side. Lorne tried the handle to the door on the right, and walked into the room that contained numerous filing cabinets and a secretary's desk that was secretary-free. Behind the desk was another door that Lorne presumed to be Tara Small's office, even though there was nothing to indicate the fact. She approached the door, gave it a brief tap, and walked in with Katy close behind her.

"Who the hell are you?" The woman was holding a hankie to her nose, but it was doing very little to stem the blood gushing from it.

"What happened?" she asked, rushing to aid the woman.

The woman held out an arm and stepped back. "Don't come near me."

Lorne persisted and handed the woman a box of tissues that had been lying on the desk. "We're trying to help. What happened?" she repeated.

The woman looked her up and down in disgust and shouted, "I fucking walked into the door, what d'ya think happened? Dumb bitch."

The venomous way the woman looked at her and addressed her made the hair stand up on the back of her neck.

Katy, who had remained by the door, said, "Calm down and tell us what went on."

"Are you two *crazy*? I know—you're from that campsite up the road, ain't ya?"

Lorne took that to mean the cardboard city community they'd spotted at the end of the road. She couldn't help laughing at the woman's absurd assumption.

"Whatcha laughing at, you dozy mare? You see me laughing?"

"I wouldn't be if I were in your shoes," Lorne said haughtily.

"Meaning?" the woman said, dabbing at her nose and replacing the bloody tissue with another from the box Lorne had given her.

Lorne raised an eyebrow. "You're looking for clarification of my statement with a nose like that? You're more stupid than you look."

The woman shoved her shoulders back and charged at Lorne, who held her position firmly. The woman, who was at least six inches taller due to the heels she was wearing, towered over her.

"You want a broken nose, too?"

Lorne laughed and turned her back on the woman and mumbled under her breath, "I'd like to see you try." Winking at Katy, who was grinning in the doorway, she said to Tara Small, "Either you tell us what happened, or I'll call the police and report the assault—it's your choice."

"No police. I don't want them here," Small snapped back before she reluctantly sat in the chair behind her desk.

Lorne and Katy exchanged knowing glances. The woman was about to open up to them; fear had that effect on people. Nevertheless, her theory was about to be proved wrong.

"I ain't tellin' you nothin' until you tell me who you are and what you're doing here."

Lorne and Katy moved to stand in front of the desk, obviously obtained from a cheap furniture store. "My husband called you at the end of last week."

"Lady, I get a lot of calls from men—hundreds every day—you wanna give me a hint what it was about?" Tara Small eyed her cautiously.

Lorne's eyes rose to the ceiling, repulsed at the thought of what the calls had entailed. "I'm a private investigator." She paused to gauge the woman's reaction, but there was none. "We're investigating a case, and the name of your agency has cropped up a few times during our investigation. If you don't mind, we'd like to ask you a few questions about the set-up you have here."

Small picked up a new tissue. "Depends."

"On what, exactly?" Lorne asked.

"Whether I want to divulge my business to some filthy P.I. or not. Go on, then, try me with one of your questions."

Small smirked, and Lorne had an idea that she was about to get the runaround. This woman appeared to know what to say and how to say it. She decided she would ease into the questions gently. "You don't mind if my colleague here takes notes, do you?"

Small shrugged. "Makes no odds to me."

"How long has the agency been open?"

"Three years," Small replied abruptly.

"And what sort of services do you offer here?"

"What services have you heard that we offer here?"

Hmmm...so you want to play cat and mouse games, do you, missy?

"It's come to our attention that you employ girls from the Far East to work as au pairs and maids."

"That's correct."

"I take it this morning's visit was from a very dissatisfied customer, then?" That rocked her. Small's eyes narrowed, and she struggled to speak for a second or two, so Lorne prompted her. "The service you provided must have been pretty bad in his eyes for him to blatantly assault you like that."

Small's gaze lowered to the desk in front of her as she mulled over Lorne's question. Then she replied quietly, "He's a business associate, not a punter."

Lorne raised a questioning eyebrow. "A business associate, huh? What's his stake in it?"

Small bristled in her seat and her back straightened in the chair. "That's my business, and I ain't tellin' ya."

Lorne turned to Katy. "Then our job is done. Ring the police, will you?"

Small shot out of her chair and tore around the desk towards Lorne. "You fucking do that, and you might as well get in touch with the undertaker at the same time."

"What do you mean?" Lorne asked, guessing what the woman meant, but needing her to confirm it from her own mouth.

"Just how stupid are you, lady? If I snitch on these guys, they'll come after me. With every torture device you can think of. You don't mess with these guys—ever."

Lorne noticed that in spite of Small's tough exterior, her hands were shaking.

"If they're that bad, then why in heaven's name did you get mixed up with them in the first place?"

"I didn't get a choice," Small said. Her shoulders slumped in defeat, she returned to her chair.

"Care to enlighten us further?"

"My business did start off legit—honest, it did. After a year or so, this guy came to see me—to *tell* me—that he was going to become my new partner."

"I see. Did he say what would happen if you refused?"

"He said he'd break every bone in my body. You kind of listen to someone when they threaten ya like that. I didn't get a choice. My business went from a legit au pair agency to a brothel and illegal people-trading business overnight. I'm the public face; any shit comes my way, like this morning. And I'll tell you this, lady: there's not a damn thing I can do about it. I'm fucked. I either do as they say, or I meet my Maker early."

"I'm sorry, Tara. That's a difficult situation to find yourself in. Is there no way you can get out?"

The woman slowly shook her head and unexpected tears welled up in her eyes. She wiped them away swiftly with the back of her bling-covered hand. "I thought about it. I even made it as far as the airport one day. I had a flight booked to Jamaica, but they got wind of it and sent two bruisers to persuade me to return. I'm stuck here as much as my girls."

"I'm sorry to hear that. Are your original girls still employed with you? Or did these guys force you to take on the girls they provided?" Lorne asked, genuinely concerned for the woman's welfare.

"Some are still with me, but others…"

"Others, what?" Lorne asked already knowing what the answer was going to be.

"Let's just say if the girls refused 'the opportunity open to them,' well…" She trailed off, brought her thumb up to her throat, and pulled it from one side to the other.

Lorne looked at Katy, who shook her head. Then she asked, "Just how many girls work for you, Tara?"

Tara shrugged. "I stopped keeping records after I reached five hundred."

"What?" Lorne asked, staggered by the figure.

"It's gone well past that number now. I wish I could get out of this stinking trade, but like I said, they won't allow it."

Katy cleared her throat. "If you're willing to testify against these men, you'll be able to get into the witness protection scheme."

"Have you not listened to a word I've said?" Small shouted at Katy.

"Of course, I have. I'm just saying, that as far as I'm concerned, that would be your only option to get out of this mess," Katy replied, incensed.

Small shot out of her chair, and Lorne positioned herself between Katy and the advancing woman. "My partner is only stating facts, Ms. Small. Now, how are we going to get you out of this mess if you're not willing to tell the police?"

The woman shrugged and shook her head as fresh tears filled her eyes, then reached for another tissue as her nose started dripping blood again. "I don't know."

"Can I ask if some of the girls live in the building?" Lorne asked, suddenly remembering what she and Katy had seen earlier.

"Yeah, there are a dozen or so of them up there."

"Is this place classed as a brothel at night?" Lorne asked, not pulling any punches now that Small appeared to be willing to cooperate with them.

Small nodded her head.

Lorne remained silent for a minute or two as she contemplated what advice she could give the woman. Without Small's willingness to involve the police—a scenario she totally understood, given the circumstances—she really didn't know what she could do to get this woman out of the terrible harm she'd been forced to put herself and her employees in. Then something sparked her brain into life: *go after the suited man.*

"The man who attacked you—what's his role in all this?"

"I told you, he's a business associate."

"Yeah, I know what you told us earlier, but in order to help you, we need more details. So…what's his role in the grand scheme of things?"

"Christ, if I told you that, my head really would be on the block. Can't you just take my word that he's involved, end of?"

"All right, I can see there's no point in pushing you. We'll take what information you've given us, have a think about things, and see if we can come up with a solution to your problem. Can you hang in there for a day or two longer?"

Small inhaled a large breath and then blew it out. "I've been involved this long; I'm sure I can handle another few days or weeks. Hell, where am I going to go. If big guys hear about your visit, I won't be here when you call back. I'll be six feet under."

CHAPTER SEVENTEEN

"Okay, I know when you're lost in thought as opposed to just being quiet for the sake of it—what gives?" Katy demanded once they had left Tara Small's office.

"Huh?"

"You heard me. Tell me what you're thinking, and while you're at it, where are we going?"

"You'll find out soon enough. Our next rendezvous is approximately five minutes away. Now, hush a minute and let me think how I'm going to tackle this, will you?" Lorne glanced Katy's way, gave her a wide smile, and winked.

Katy's arms folded across her chest and she let out an exasperated breath. "Whatever."

"As soon as we get to our location, all will become much clearer—I hope," she added apprehensively after voicing her statement aloud.

"Huh. Not only was my birthday weekend spoilt, but now the lady wants to torture me by keeping me in suspense," Katy mumbled.

Lorne couldn't help laughing at her ex-partner, who, at the moment, was acting more like her daughter.

"Well, I'm glad you find me amusing," Katy added sarcastically.

"Patience, dear girl, patience."

A few minutes later, Lorne reached their intended destination. She pulled into the long drive and parked outside the main entrance to the house, noting that there were two cars already sitting in the drive.

Katy whistled. "Wow! Looks like someone's numbers came up on the lottery."

"Come on, you. Leave the talking to me this time, all right?"

"Aww, I kind of liked winding Small up back there."

"Yeah, and you nearly got a smack in the mouth for your trouble. Seriously, we need to tread carefully here, hon. One question."

"Shoot," Katy replied, baffled.

"Do you have your warrant card with you, or did you have to hand it in when you were suspended?"

"Damn. You know what—I forgot to hand it in to Roberts," Katy replied, feigning regret.

"Good. Let's go."

As they approached the house, Lorne raised her hand to use the ornate knocker, but before she could reach it, the door was yanked open and the person she least wanted or expected to find there glared down at her. "What the fuck do you want?"

"Hello, Mr. North, it's nice to see you again so soon," Lorne replied breezily, hoping her words had managed to mask Katy's surprised gasp.

"My wife can't see you at present; you'll have to call back another time," he said angrily, his gaze going over Lorne's shoulder, causing her to warily look behind her. *Is he expecting someone?*

She smiled her sweetest smile. "Why can't Angela see us, Mr. North?"

His focus pulled back to Lorne and seemed to pierce her soul. "She's indisposed. Actually, she's getting ready to go to one of her damn charity luncheons, if you must know."

Lorne walked up the step and heard Katy do the same behind her. "I'm sure she won't mind if we come in and wait for her. I told her that we would keep her up to date with the case."

He tried to shut the door in her face, but Lorne shouldered it open. Caught off-guard, North staggered backwards, allowing Lorne and Katy to storm through to the lounge where they found Angela sitting in her winged chair reading a book. The startled woman glanced up and gulped. Her eyes fluttered shut, as if she feared trouble ahead.

"Angela, what the hell happened to you?" Lorne was shocked to see the amount of bruising covering the woman's face, despite the heavy makeup she was wearing.

"Oh, that. I had an accident the other day. It's nothing to worry about, dear, really," Angela said. Her gaze dropped back down to the book in her lap, as though she were ashamed of the obvious lie she had just told.

"If you don't mind leaving now, my wife needs her rest." North was standing in front of his wife, and Lorne noticed how Angela flinched every time his arms moved.

Instead of leaving, Lorne turned to wink at Katy and motioned with a nod for her to sit down on the sofa. After she and Katy were settled, Lorne said, "I realise you're a busy man, Mr. North, please don't let us interfere with your work. We'll keep Angela company for a little while."

His eyes widened, and Lorne saw his mouth moving as though he were grinding his teeth.

"My work can wait."

Damn! With things not exactly going to plan, Lorne decided to try another tack. "It's unusual for you to be at home during the week, isn't it, Mr. North?"

"So? I'm not sure what you're insinuating."

Lorne smiled at him. "I was just wondering if you usually worked from home."

"Occasionally."

"When you opened the door for us, you appeared to be expecting someone else—can I ask who?"

North stepped around his wife and placed his arm on the mantelpiece. "Why would it concern you?"

Lorne pulled her trump card. "Would it have anything to do with the visit you made to Tara Small this morning?"

He glared at her and thought for a moment or two before he responded. "What if it has?"

Lorne turned to Angela, and as much as she wanted to keep her out of the conversation, she found herself asking, "Are you aware of your husband's business dealings, Angela?"

The woman twisted in her seat uncomfortably, which worried Lorne. *Is she hurting? Or does she know of her husband's activities?*

"Angela?" she prompted.

When the woman remained silent, she went down considerably in Lorne's estimation. But she didn't understand. If she knew about his other business, why had she openly given Lorne the agency's number and address? What the heck was she playing at? Was it some sort of cry for help?

"I'll ask you again, Angela: where did you get those bruises?"

The woman's gaze immediately shot up to her husband. North appeared to be challenging her to keep her mouth shut. Lorne left her seat and went over to Angela. She knelt down beside her and took the woman's trembling hands in her own. "Angela, he won't hurt you anymore, I promise."

North lunged at Lorne, but Katy was quick to stop him from reaching her. Katy flipped him over her hip, North lay prostrate on the floor with Katy's knee pressed into his chest. "Wrong move, pal."

"Sorry, I forgot to introduce you to DS Katy Foster."

"Fucking get off me, you bitch. You'll never work for the police again by the time my solicitor has wiped the floor with you. You say anything, Angela, and I swear I'll…" He left his threat dangling dangerously.

Angela looked at her and gave a brief smile. "My husband…has several vices…that I am no longer comfortable with," she stuttered.

"Like beating up women, you mean?" Lorne pressed her.

With her husband being restricted by Katy, Angela's courage visibly grew. "Among other things, yes. I no longer want to be part of his sickening world, but when I voiced my worries the other day, he beat me until I couldn't get up." Then she surprised Lorne by kicking her husband in the ribs. "Didn't you?"

"You deserved it, bitch. You do as I say or suffer the consequences—"

Lorne squeezed Angela's hand. "Spoken like a true man. Angela, if you want this stopped, you know you'll have to make a complaint to the police, don't you?"

"You wouldn't *dare*," North warned his wife before Katy twisted his arm higher up his back. He grunted and spat at her.

Katy kneed North in the ribs, and he grunted again like the pig he was portraying himself to be. "Nah, Lorne, he ain't nice at all. Mrs. North, you have to make a complaint. I'll willingly accompany you to the station."

"I'm not so sure. If I could get away from him, I would; however, the last thing I want to do is leave my beautiful home, and *his* son, Anthony, needs me," Angela stated sadly, as if it had just dawned on her with an almighty force that she was stuck with this despicable man.

Lorne knew that when it came to the crunch, abused women constantly changed their minds.

Roger North snorted and earned himself another jab from Katy's knee.

"That's your choice, Angela, but I want to take Jai San away from this environment. Where is she, by the way?"

Angela nodded. "I understand. She's in her room, I believe."

"Will you be all right here for a minute, Katy, while I go and fetch her?"

"Sure, although I could do with a better padded seat than this bony bastard."

Lorne left the room to the sound of North berating Katy, calling her every vile name he could think of in between crying out in pain from Katy's retaliation.

She ran up the stairs and followed the soft sound of music playing. She tapped on the door where she thought the music was coming from and walked into the room uninvited. Jai San was sitting cross-legged on the floor of a small bedroom, which consisted of only a single bed and a small wardrobe. The young woman looked alarmed when she saw Lorne walk into the room. She scampered onto the bed and placed a pillow in front of her.

"Jai San, I was here the other day, remember? I've come to help you. Don't be scared." She eased into the room and toward the girl, who was now visibly trembling. "You, poor thing. Did Mr. North do this to you?" Lorne traced a gentle finger down the left side of her face, which was swollen and looked very painful.

Ashamed, Jai San's gaze drifted to the bed beside her. Lorne sat down on the end of the bed and stroked her leg. "He's not going to hurt you again, sweetie, I won't let him. Can you pack a bag quickly? You're coming with me."

Jai San pulled away from her and vigorously shook her head. "No, can't do that. He *owns* me. If I go, he says he hurt my family back home. Please, leave me alone."

Lorne blew out a breath. "Sweetheart, I have a policewoman downstairs who is actually sitting on top of Mr. North at this moment." The image brought a smile to both of their faces. "I'll do everything in my power to make sure he won't hurt either you or your family again. Now pack a bag, please."

Jai San hurled herself off the bed and threw what few clothes she had into a couple of carrier bags she found folded up in the bottom of her wardrobe.

Lorne watched her, her mind racing as she tried to figure out how Jai San and her family were all going to fit into her medium-sized home. *I'll make them fit. There's no way I'm leaving this girl here!*

Once she'd finished packing her sorrowful looking bags, Jai San announced cheerfully, "I ready now, miss."

Lorne rubbed her arm as she passed her. "Then let's go. I hope you like animals."

"Oh, yes, miss, very much."

Lorne's heart swelled with joy at the relief displayed on the young woman's face to be getting out of this situation. "When I was a child, my family used to raise goats for milk to sell at the market, before we moved to the city."

"You'll be back there soon, Jai San, I'll see to that."

They ran down the stairs and into the lounge, but came to an abrupt halt in the doorway.

What the fuck?

The three people Lorne had left in the lounge had been joined by another man. He had Katy in front of him, one arm locked around her throat while the other arm waved a knife a few inches in front of her face. Lorne had never seen Katy look so scared.

"Ah, glad you could rejoin us, Lorne. Do come in. As you can see, circumstances have changed somewhat since you left us."

She eyed North through a narrowed, untrusting glare. "What's going on? Who are you?" she asked, turning to the man holding Katy hostage.

His amusement of the situation was clear to see, the man ignored her, probably under instruction that he leave all the talking to North.

North laughed and eyed Lorne with contempt. "You think you had this all worked out, didn't you, bitch?"

"Not at all. What exactly is 'all this,' anyway?" she asked, her hand moving to her jacket pocket where her mobile was.

But North bellowed at her, "Stop right there, Warner—or is it Simpkins? Word has it that when you were in the Met, you were one of the feistiest cops around. Let's see how you fucking get out of this mess, shall we?"

"Let Katy go and we'll talk."

"And you have a right to order me around because…?" North challenged, smirking.

Arsehole, you weren't smirking just a minute ago when Katy had you flat out on the floor. Lorne took a tentative step further into the room in North's direction, and he took two steps to his right, which placed him a few feet from his wife. Out of the corner of her eye, she saw Jai San shrink back and heard her expel a terrified breath.

"Let's talk about this like adults, shall we? Let's all sit down nice and relaxed."

North gave a derisive laugh. "In your world everything might be fluffy and dandy, but in mine, you've poked your nose into my business, cost me time, and, more importantly, money. I don't take meddling of that proportion lightly. Do I, Sansom?"

The man latched onto his meaning instantly and ran the pointed tip of the knife down Katy's left cheek. Katy cried out and tried to escape the man's grasp, but he held firm around her neck and her struggling turned out to be in vain.

Lorne's gut clenched tightly. "Stop! Don't hurt her anymore, please."

"*Don't hurt her anymore, please!*" North mimicked, a smile tugging at his thin mouth.

Lorne's gaze dropped down to Angela, who was sitting on the edge of her winged chair, and she pleaded silently for some kind of help, but the woman looked away. *Shit! How the hell do I get us out of this mess? Tony, where are you when I need you most?*

North dropped down into a crouch beside his wife, and Angela flinched at his closeness. "Now, my dear, Sansom and I are going to take these nice ladies for a ride in his van. You're going to stay right here in this chair until I return, do you hear me?"

"Yes," Angela muttered in response.

Her husband's hand gripped her knee, and Angela's eyes instantly squeezed shut. "Look at me," North ordered, and his wife's eyes flew open. "I can't hear you. I said, do you hear me? If I find you missing when I get back, you *know* what will happen. That sister of yours will need to be pushed down the aisle in a wheelchair in a few weeks."

Angela's hand shot to her chest. "You wouldn't!"

North tilted his head. "Wouldn't I?" Turning to Sansom, he asked, "I take it you have rope in that van of yours?"

"Yep, in the passenger's seat. Want me to go and get it?"

"No, I'll go. You watch these." North stood up, strode past Lorne and out through the front entrance.

Lorne looked at Katy and raised her left eyebrow, silently asking if she was up for a fight or not. Katy opened and closed her eyes three times in response—it was a signal they had worked out back when they were real partners. Then Katy lashed out, digging her right elbow into Sansom's side. Despite Katy's elbow connecting heavily with his ribs, his arm held tightly around her neck, limiting any further movement on her part, and she began to choke due to the pressure he was exerting on her windpipe.

It was Lorne's turn to make her move. She ran at the man, but stopped dead in her tracks when Sansom raised the knife and turned it inwards toward Katy's chest. Both Angela and Jai San screamed. Lorne held up her hands in defeat. "Sorry, Katy."

"We tried, Lorne."

Hearing the commotion coming from inside the house, North came sprinting back into the room, looking angrier than when he'd left it. He strode up to Lorne and stood in front of her. Her gaze latched on to his and she neglected to see the back of his hand coming her way. She cried out as his hand connected with her cheek and sent her off-balance. The force flung her sideways, and she landed on the couch. "Dumb, bitch. That'll teach you to try your superwoman antics with me. You won't be so fucking foolish the next time, will you?"

Lorne put her cool hand to her blazing cheek and winced at the harsh lesson she'd just been handed. *Bide your time, girl. Let him think he's dealing with an amateur, and then pounce when he's least expecting it. If the opportunity ever arises.*

Lorne, Katy, and Jai San were tied up with their hands behind their backs and taken out to the van one by one. Sansom took Katy out first and stayed with her while North took Jai San and then Lorne out of the house. Between North taking Jai San and returning to fetch Lorne, whom North had tied to a heavy bureau, she begged with Angela a final time to reconsider helping them. "Please, Angela. You don't have to go to the police—just ring my husband, that's all I ask," Lorne said, desperation lingering in her voice.

"I can't! There's my sister to consider. You heard what he said." Tears of frustration welled up in Angela's eyes and Lorne nodded her understanding. She totally understood the woman's dreadful predicament. But, if Angela couldn't or wouldn't help them, then who would?

CHAPTER EIGHTEEN

After being thrown into the back of the van, almost crushing each other, there was a slight delay before the van moved off while Samson dumped Katy's car in a nearby lane. North sat on the one seat available in the back, glaring at his captives.

Lorne glanced at Katy with an expression that said, 'we're in deep shit now, girl.' Inhaling a large breath and wishing she hadn't after filling her lungs with the fumes from an oily cloth lying next to her, Lorne asked, "Where are you taking us?"

"Ever the inquisitive one. You'll see when you get there. We're going to teach you a lesson or two about how not to interfere in my lucrative business." North sneered at her and then turned his attention to Jai San.

The young woman was shaking violently now. Lorne feared she knew what lay ahead of her. Something they'd all be finding out soon enough. She wished she still had her mobile phone in her pocket; she could have figured out the number pad through the cloth and opened up a line so Tony could listen in to what was happening to them. But North and Sansom had frisked her and Katy and removed both their mobiles before they'd bundled them into the back of the van.

They must have been travelling for about twenty to twenty-five minutes before they arrived at their destination. From her obscure position, Lorne caught brief glimpses of the area, she knew exactly where they were. Her stomach twisted and turned itself in large knots.

Katy nudged Lorne's foot and mouthed, "We're at the warehouse."

Sansom jumped out to open the gates, with North distracted watching the driver Lorne nodded at Katy. "I know." Her heart sank as the driver got back in the van and pulled it into the yard.

"Here we are, *ladies*—I use the term loosely, of course. It's time to see what you're really made of." North moved to the rear of the van and waited for the doors to open. They heard the gates clang shut and then the doors sprang open. Jai San was the first to be yanked from the vehicle. She was crying and shaking uncontrollably. The two men merely laughed at the young woman, and then North disappeared with her.

"What the fuck are we going to do, Lorne?" Katy whispered.

North reappeared before Lorne could answer her. He grabbed Katy's leg and hauled her out of the back of the van, she landed on the concrete with a sickening *thump*. Katy—being Katy—refused to cry out in pain. Lorne felt proud of her, and hoped that she would be able to remain strong throughout the torment that she imagined lay ahead of them.

Lorne twisted and turned in the confined space, trying to get into a better position to avoid going through the same as Katy when North came to collect her. He rounded the open door and his mouth turned up into a knowing smile. "You're a quick learner. I'm going to enjoy teaching *you* most of all."

"Bastard! You lay a finger on either of us, and I swear you'll live to regret it." Just in case North knew who the Unicorn was, she added, "A few years ago, a man in the same line of business as you, paid the ultimate price when he kidnapped my daughter."

"Ah, the lioness has roared. I'd better watch out for those nasty claws of yours, hadn't I?" North laughed callously. He pulled her out of the van, shoved her in the back to make her walk in front of him and into the warehouse.

Inside, the other two girls had been locked in a cage. A quick scan of the area told Lorne that they were alone, and the other girls they had witnessed being brought here had already been shipped out to God knew where.

North threw Lorne behind bars with the others, and then he and Sansom moved away from the cage to hold a whispered conversation, which ended with both men laughing loudly. Then the two men returned and stood in front of the cage, eyeing Lorne and the other two captives with pure lust in their beady eyes.

North approached the cage door and opened it, stepping through the doorway and walking over to where Lorne was standing. His eyes ran the length of her body, and under his creepy gaze, she struggled to prevent the shudder running up her spine. Her shoulders straightened in determination and as North's gaze met hers, she spat at him, hitting him directly between the eyes.

Angered by the insult, North swiped her across the face again. However, this time Lorne had prepared herself for the strike, and remained bolt upright.

"You'll pay for that, Warner. First, you're going to watch what we do to the other two, and then I'll have pleasure in teaching you how to behave around men. Obviously it's a talent lacking in your extensive repertoire." North's gaze remained on Lorne as he reached out and found Jai San's arm.

The young woman screamed as North led her from the cage and locked the door behind them.

"Shit! Katy, what are we going to do?"

"My advice half an hour ago would have been not to antagonize him, but I think it's too late for that."

"Shit!" Lorne said for a second time as they observed the two men pushing the girl between them. Each time she left the arms of one man, they heard her clothes tear, until finally Jai San stood naked between the two men. Lorne tried to turn away, desperate not to see what the girl was about to be subjected to, but she felt that if she did that, Jai San would feel she had deserted her.

North forced Jai San to bend over and placed her face near his open fly while Sansom dropped his trousers and entered the woman from behind. North fiddled with his crotch and exposed his erect penis, then forced it into Jai San's mouth. The terror and humiliation that haunted the young woman's eyes tore at Lorne's heart, yet she was thankful that Jai San didn't put up a fight. Had she resisted, the punishment would have been ten times worse. *Is this what she's had to put up with every day of her life since she turned up on the Norths' doorstep?*

Bile rose and burned the back of her throat. "Fuck!"

She heard Katy gag and spit on the floor next to her. "I can't...I won't let them do that to me, Lorne," she said through gritted teeth.

"I'm not sure you're going to have a choice, Katy," Lorne said reluctantly. She searched the cage for any form of sharp edge with which to cut the rope tying her hands, but came up blank.

She heaved when she saw North shoot his load in Jai San's mouth at the same time that Sansom reached his climax. Thinking they'd finished with Jai San, Lorne was devastated when they threw the girl on her back and North dived on top of her. She couldn't watch anymore and shut her eyes, but she could do nothing to block out Jai San's pitiful cries for help.

Oh God, what have we done to deserve this?

CHAPTER NINETEEN

Tony was anxiously pacing the floor with one of the pups in his arms when Sam walked into the kitchen.

"Something wrong?"

"It's Lorne. She said she would ring me throughout the morning—you know, after the scare she had with that lunatic trying to drive her off the road the other day," Tony replied. He bent down and placed the pup gently beside its siblings, then sat down at the table.

Sam sat beside him and thumped his upper arm gently. "This is my daughter we're talking about, Tony. She'll be fine—you know she will. Has Katy gone with her?"

"Yes. It doesn't alter the fact that she told me she'd call in and hasn't, Sam. If Lorne says she's going to call me, she always—*always*—sticks to it."

"Okay, let's think logically about this. She was going to the agency first thing, wasn't she?" Sam asked.

"Yep. I have no way of knowing if she turned up there or not. Her phone is switched off."

Sam looked up at the clock on the wall; it was almost midday. "Maybe she hit trouble there. Can you ring the agency?"

Tony nodded. "I have. There was no answer. Which, again, doesn't bode well."

"Now, don't go thinking anything bad has happened to Lorne and Katy. Let's get the facts sorted out first. It might be wise if you took a trip over there."

"I can't leave this place. The pups need feeding every few hours, and we have some visitors coming here this afternoon to view some of the long-term boarders—"

Sam held up a hand to stop him. "I can look after things around here."

"But Lorne said I wasn't to trouble you because you weren't feeling well," Tony replied, concerned.

"Here's the plan: we'll have some lunch, and then if she hasn't made contact with us by one o'clock, I want you to go over to the agency and see what you can find out. Deal?"

"Deal. Thanks, Sam."

The next hour flew past as Tony threw himself into his chores and wolfed down the sandwich Sam made him. When he still hadn't heard from Lorne by the agreed time, he bid Sam goodbye, picked up the keys to the van, and set off for the agency.

During the journey, his mind sought through the numerous questions he was going to ask the woman at the agency when he laid eyes on her.

At one forty-five, he parked the rescue centre's van outside the agency and ran up the steps. Although he wanted to barge into the woman's office and demand to know where Lorne and Katy were, he took a few deep breaths to calm himself and knocked gently on the agency door. The outer office was empty, so he knocked on the second door.

"Come in," came a woman's abrupt response.

Tony entered the room and instantly frowned at the woman sitting at the desk. "Tara Small?"

"Yeah, who wants to know?" she asked cautiously.

Tony approached the desk and extended his hand. The woman stared at it, totally disinterested. "Tony Warner."

"And? Should that name mean anything to me? You mind getting to the point?" She paused to look down at the papers spread across her desk. "I'm kind of busy here."

Tony moved around to the side of the desk, and that was when something caught his eye. In the wastepaper basket, he saw a handful of bloody tissues. *Time to stop being the nice guy and start getting the answers I need.*

"Have you had an accident?"

Small's brow wrinkled in confusion. "What?"

He pointed down at the bin in front of him.

"Oh that. It was nothing. What do you want, Mr. Warner?"

Tony leaned on the desk placing his face a few inches from hers. "My wife."

Small shot back in her chair. "You've lost your wife and need one of my girls to fill her shoes, is that it?" she queried perplexed.

"Is it fuck! You know damn well who I am and why I'm here. Now where's my bloody wife?"

The woman got out of her chair to challenge him. "How the fuck should I know, you creep? She left here hours ago. Maybe she's desperate to get away from you harassing her."

"I'll ask you one more time before I force you to tell me."

Tara Small's hand opened the drawer to her desk and disappeared inside. She pulled out a small-bladed knife and thrust it in front of Tony's face. "Bring it on, big boy."

Tony backed up, ensuring the desk wouldn't hamper his next move. He held his hands up and shrugged. "Okay, you win."

As soon as Tara's hand relaxed its grip on the blade, his arm shot out and gave her forearm a karate chop. Shocked to see the blade fly out of her hand she backed up towards the wall behind her. "I don't want any trouble—I've had enough of that for one day."

"What the fuck do you mean by that?" Tony moved around the desk and saw her eyes widen in fear. "I have no intention of hurting you. Just tell me where my wife is."

"I have no idea. I told you, she left here hours ago. I have no idea what people do after they leave these premises."

"What trouble have you had today? What's with the blood-soaked tissues?"

Small shrugged and her eyes drifted down to the wastepaper basket. "An unhappy associate caught me off-guard this morning."

"Nice business you run here, if that's how an associate treats you. Was this before or after Lorne visited you this morning?"

"Before. I repeat: I have no idea where she went after leaving here," Small told him, appearing to relax a little.

"Answer me this: why would an associate attack you like that? I presume that's what happened."

"Because I'm in the wrong line of business, I guess. Like your wife suggested. Please, you have to leave. They watch this place and the punters who come here. If you stay around too long, more trouble will land on my doorstep."

"Okay, but first you need to tell me who this associate is," Tony said, thinking what Lorne would've asked the woman and where her next line of questioning would have likely taken her.

"I can't. I'm sorry."

Tony pinned the woman against the wall. "No more Mr. Nice Guy, lady. Tell me who the associate is—now."

Small's arms tried to release Tony's forearm from pinching her throat but her efforts proved to be useless. In a croaky voice, she gave him the name. "Roger North."

Tony stepped back, and Small immediately rubbed at her neck. "Have you got an address for him?"

Small shook her head warily. "No, only a mobile number."

"Let me have it."

Small scrolled through the Rolodex on her desk, plucked out a card, and handed it to Tony. He wrote down the number on a pad and then pocketed the piece of paper.

"Thanks for your help. For your sake and mine, you'd be wise to keep your mouth shut about my visit."

Small nodded her understanding and Tony left the office. The first thing he did was ring Lorne's father. "Sam, Lorne and Katy left the agency hours ago. The woman had a visit from one of her associates who attacked her."

"Shit. What are you going to do now, Tony?"

"Here's the thing: the associate was Roger North. Angela North's husband."

"Please tell me you're on your way to his house."

"That was my intention, yes. I've only got a mobile number for him, though. Can you check in the diary for the address? I'm sure Lorne wrote it in there. If she didn't, can you give Jade a call? Try the diary first; I don't want to cause Jade any unnecessary concern at this point."

"Righto, hold on a mo'."

Tony drummed his fingers on the steering wheel while he waited.

"Here you go." Lorne's father relayed the address and then said, "Let me know what happens when you get there, Tony. Be careful."

"Just as a precaution, if you don't hear from me within the next hour, call the police and send them to the Norths' house."

"I'll do that."

Tony hung up and pressed his foot down hard on the accelerator.

He pulled into the drive and knocked on the front door. Receiving no answer, Tony took the path around the side of the house. When he reached the back of the house, he looked through the French doors and was surprised to find a middle-aged woman sitting in a winged chair with her arms wrapped around her knees. He tapped lightly on the French doors and she leapt out of her seat in fright.

She wiped away the tears that glistened on her cheek, her voice shook when she shouted, "Who are you and what do you want?"

"Sorry, I didn't mean to scare you. I'm looking for my wife, Lorne Warner."

The woman quickly ran to the door and pushed it back. "Oh thank God. I didn't know what to do…my husband will kill me if he finds out…but those poor women."

"Whoa! Now hold on a minute; you're not making sense. Has Lorne been here today?"

"Yes…yes, she was here with another woman several hours ago."

"So they left. Do you know where they went?" Tony felt relieved, but then the fear emanating from the woman's eyes warned him not to count his chickens just yet.

She collapsed back into the chair and averted her eyes. "They all left."

"You're not making any sense. Who?"

"My husband and his *friend* took the three girls."

Tony's heart rate spiked and his mouth suddenly went dry. "Who do you mean by three girls?"

"Sorry, I mean women. Lorne, Jai San, and your wife's friend. They're in terrible danger. He's going to kill them. I wanted to ring you, but he threatened to hurt my sister if I contacted you," Angela said in between sobs.

"Where have they taken them?"

"I don't know. All this is a shock to me. I knew my husband had a violent streak, but I never dreamed he could be caught up in something like this."

"You must have an address or something that will lead me to where they have Lorne—please?"

Angela shook her head in frustration. "I don't, I swear. As far as I knew, my husband worked in the city as an accountant. Imagine my horror when I discovered he was involved in this dreadful business. Why? Why would he do that to these girls? It's barbaric. Lorne asked me to tell the police. He'd already beat me to a bloody pulp. He'd kill me if I called anyone, but I've been sitting here thinking about how these poor women are suffering, and I can't allow it to happen anymore."

"I'll call a friend of mine. You can trust him to help you out of this mess and into protective custody."

"Would you?"

Tony rang DCI Sean Roberts and explained the situation to him.

"Christ, Tony! I'll send a couple of my men over. Do you need any help trying to track Lorne down?"

"Yeah, it would help if you got your guys to keep an eye out for them on the streets. We have no idea where… Hold on a minute."

"Tony? What is it?"

"The warehouse. I bet he's taken them there." Tony gave Sean the location and asked him to send a couple of squad cars out to the location.

Tony hung up and asked Angela, "Will you be okay by yourself? Is there anyone you can contact to come and sit with you until the police arrive?"

She nodded. "My neighbour can pop over, if you think it's safe for her to do so."

"That I can't guarantee. Maybe you should go to her house. The police are on their way; odds are they'll be here within ten minutes or so."

"I'll see you out and then go and see her. Thank you, and I'm so sorry about your wife. She's a brave lady."

Before Tony could ask her what she meant, his mobile rang. "Hello?"

"Tony, thank God. It's Carol Lang."

Tony gave Angela a brief wave and then got into his car. He watched the woman disappear through an archway in her hedge, then turned his attention back to Carol. "Sorry, Carol. I'm kind of in a rush."

"I know, dear, and rush, you must. I fell asleep in the chair after lunch and woke up with a start. Lorne's deceased partner, Pete, contacted me—can you believe that? The cynic of all cynics contacting me."

Tony sighed heavily. "Carol, please get on with it, Lorne's life is in danger."

"I know, I know. He told me. What he said was a little hazy, so bear with me."

"I'm listening." Tony fidgeted in his seat and started the engine.

"He gave me tall railings. Huge buildings. Busy during the day, but silent at night," Carol told him.

"The warehouse. I had the same inkling. Thanks, Carol, that reinforces my idea."

He put the van into gear and released the handbrake, ready to drive off, but what Carol said next made him shudder. "Tony, *listen* to me. Lorne is in mortal danger. She's no longer at the warehouse."

"Then where the fuck is she?" Tony demanded. He slapped the palm of his hand across the steering wheel.

"I don't know, dear. I wish I did. Would you like me to come over to the house? Something might come to me, and we'll be able to act upon it straight away if I'm there with you."

"I'm out and about, Carol. Sam's back at the house, if you want to go over there. I think I'll go and take a look at the warehouse just in case. Not that I don't believe you, but I might find something over there that'll tell me where they've taken Lorne and Katy."

"My goodness, Katy is with her, too? Pete didn't tell me there was anyone else involved. I'll get over to your house as soon as I possibly can. Does Sam know?"

"He knows that Lorne is missing, yes. He's feeling under the weather lately, so it might be a good idea if one of us was back there with him. Thanks, Carol. I'll ring the house if I find anything out."

The next call he made was to Sam. It was of the hardest calls he had ever had to prepare himself for, and throughout the call, his foot kept moving up and down on the accelerator, making the inside of the van far noisier than normal. At times, Sam had to ask him to repeat himself, which only twisted Tony's gut ten times harder.

"Sam, listen to me: it'll be all right. I'm going to contact a couple of friends of mine. We'll hunt the bastards down if we have to. I'll make them regret the day they ever messed with either Lorne or myself—that's if she hasn't done that already."

"I am listening, Tony, but being the more cautious amongst us, it won't stop me from worrying. You say that Carol is on her way over here?" Sam asked.

Tony noticed that during their conversation Sam's voice had faltered a few times. He hated giving him the unfortunate news over the phone, but keeping the news from Lorne's father was a definite no-no. They had all made a pact when the business had started up that they would tell each other the truth, no matter how harsh that truth turned out to be.

Tony watched a car pull into the drive. Two men in suits got out and walked his way. "That's right, Sam. Look, I better go. The police have just turned up at North's house. I need to have a word with them before I shoot off."

"Keep me informed, Tony."

"I will. See you later."

Tony wound down the window and told the plain-clothed officers that Angela North had just gone next door to her neighbour's house. He gave a brief rundown of what had happened and suggested that the officers take Angela to the station for her protection, at least for the time being.

The officers agreed and Tony left. On the way, he called an MI5 agent who had helped them out in the past.

"Hey, Weir, how's it hanging?"

"Warner?" The man laughed. "It's hanging like a donkey's, as usual, mate. Not seen any action for months, though, so it'll be shrivelling up soon enough. Long time no hear. Where have you been?"

Tony gave a brief laugh at the man's joke and then reprimanded himself as guilt swept through him. "I've been around, as they say. Listen, man, I'm in a pickle. Any chance either you or Taylor could help me out on the sly?"

Weir's voice lowered. "I think we both need to get out of here for a while; the bloody new boss is driving us nuts. Tell me where and when and we'll meet you."

Relieved, Tony punched the air. He gave Weir the address to the warehouse and warned him not to do anything until he got there. "We'll hit it by force, together."

"In the daylight?" Weir asked surprised.

"If we have to, yes. I'll see you later."

CHAPTER TWENTY

Approximately thirty minutes later, Tony parked a few roads away from the warehouse. Unlike the last time he had been here with Lorne, the industrial estate was a thriving and noisy community. Hearing a car door slam behind him, he looked in his rearview mirror and saw two men walking toward the van—Weir and Taylor.

They opened the passenger's door, Taylor hopped in the back, and Weir sat in the front seat. "Nice wheels," Weir said sarcastically.

"It does the job. Thanks for coming, guys. The warehouse is around the corner. Last time we were here, the gates, which are like ten feet high, were locked."

"Have you been to check what the situation is now?" Taylor asked.

Tony shook his head. "Nope, I arrived two minutes ago, thought I'd wait for you guys to get here before proceeding."

Weir spoke next. "Well, I suggest one of us—either Taylor or myself—ambles by pretending we're looking for a specific company in the vicinity. Taylor, are you up for it?"

"No probs. On foot, or shall I take the car?"

"Foot would be better," Tony told him.

Weir let Taylor out and they watched him walk around the corner and out of sight. Neither man spoke again until he returned five minutes later.

This time, Weir jumped in the back and Taylor sat in the passenger's seat. "Couldn't see a lot because the gates were shut. I suggest we drive 'round the back of the building, maybe take the next road down, and see if we can gain entry into the unit from there without drawing too much attention to ourselves. The road at the front of the building is far too busy to attempt anything."

"Good idea," Tony said. He started the engine, reversed up, and drove down the next road.

Weir suggested, "Drive past, Tony, so we can suss it out first."

There was no convenient opening in the fence that they could get through as far as Tony could see. He pulled the car in and the three of them left the vehicle. Taylor was right; this road appeared to be the final one to the estate and was indeed far quieter than any of the others.

"How are we going to handle this?" Weir glanced down at Tony's false leg to emphasise his meaning.

Tony slapped his thigh. "Don't go worrying about this guy, he's capable of doing anything yours can do and then some."

"Right," Weir said, seemingly taking charge of the situation. "I'll give you a leg up. Er…excuse the pun."

Tony tutted good-naturedly and thrust his good leg into Weir's linked hands. He climbed up the spiked fence, thankfully clearing the top without causing any damage to either himself or his clothes. Tony snuck up behind the warehouse and waited for the other two men to join him.

"It looks deserted to me," Taylor said. He reached inside his jacket and pulled out a crowbar. "Let's go."

Taylor went first. He pried the door open and beckoned the others to follow him.

Tony's nose wrinkled in repulsion. "Jesus! What's that smell?"

"He's definitely been out of the game too long," Weir said as he moved further into the building. "That, my dear friend, is the smell of fear, mixed with the smell of sex."

Tony felt his stomach lurch and the colour drain from his face. *Hold it together, man.*

Taylor gave him a dig in the ribs. "You all right? Don't you go cracking up on us."

Tony sucked in a breath to calm himself and regretted it. He spat out the bile that burned his throat and nodded at Taylor. "I'm all right. Let's do this."

They searched the caged area first and found discarded, torn female clothes. Thankfully, Tony didn't recognise any belonging to his wife. The stench coming off the thin mattresses lying on the floor had intensified to the extent that none of them stayed in the area long.

Taylor pointed to another section of the warehouse near the rear and the three of them went over to investigate. Fresh blood pooled on the floor alongside a thin white blouse that had been shredded to pieces and a black pair of women's trousers in the same state. "This looks as if it took place recently," Taylor said, wincing as he spoke.

Tony kicked out at a nearby crate. "Shit! Where the fuck is she? The specifics we have on the case so far are that any girls shipped into the country are brought here and then dispatched around the country. We haven't found any concrete evidence as yet to where these girls end up. We know an agency is involved, but the owner is being uncooperative. She got beat up by an associate only this morning; to me, that could mean that their partnership has altered in some way, and she wasn't keen to dish the dirt. Who's to say where these women would end up next? Or, more to the point, where Lorne and Katy will end up."

Weir shrugged. "I don't know what to say, mate. We can hunt around here for hours, but I doubt if we're going to come up with anything new. I'm not sure what to suggest."

Taylor nodded. "He's right. Our hands are tied right now, Tony. Until something else surfaces, that is."

"Okay, let's get out of here," Tony said, his shoulders slouching despondently.

Weir shoved him in the back as he followed him to the door. "Hey, where's that stiff upper lip gone? From what I've seen of her, Lorne will have her wits about her. Keep the faith, mate."

After climbing the fence and dropping the two agents back at their car, Tony headed back home. There was nothing else he could do.

* * *

Lorne struggled to keep upright in the back of the van. The driver had his foot down and didn't seem to be taking the other people in the vehicle into consideration as he swerved around the corners of the narrow lanes. Even North shouted and cussed at him to slow down from his seat in the back.

Another corner, and Lorne crushed Jai San yet again. Fighting to sit back up, she smiled an apology at the young woman. The woman's face was blank, devoid of all emotion. Lorne noticed how dead her eyes looked since her ordeal. Her heart went out to her.

Once the men had finished with Jai San, they had thrust her into the cage. She'd landed at Lorne's feet, naked and trembling. Lorne sat on the floor and using her feet had tried to put one of the smelly blankets around Jai San's quivering shoulders. With Lorne distracted, the men had seized their opportunity to grab Katy and pull her out of the cage. Amidst perverse laughter, they had dragged the screaming and kicking Katy over to the other side of the warehouse. However, before either of the men could hurt her, North had received a call on his mobile. The call had angered North, he threw some soiled clothes at Jai San and ordered her to get dressed before the three women had been roughly loaded back in the van once more.

On the way to a destination unknown, Lorne had surmised one thing from the call North had received: he was taking orders from someone else. Bang went her theory of thinking he was the man in charge of this gang. At that moment, Lorne's fear for their safety escalated to a new level. Fear of the unknown had always been her downfall. *Please, Tony, help us!*

Lorne eyed Katy with concern; Katy, too, had been quiet since her near-miss ordeal. She nudged her foot with her own to get her attention, but Katy refused to look at her. *Is she blaming me for getting her involved in this case?* She tried again, harder this time, but Katy still averted her eyes.

North caught the movement out of the corner of his eye. "I told you to keep still," he said and struck Lorne hard across the face.

Blood instantly filled her mouth, Lorne spat it out and he laughed. Defiantly, she said, "Your bullying won't wash with me, North. I'm biding my time."

"Your pathetic threats won't wash with me, Warner." He hit her again for good measure on the other side of her face. "There—now you have a matching pair." He threw his head back and laughed.

Lorne glanced over at Katy, who was shaking her head in disappointment. Lorne's chin dropped to her chest as the realisation dawned on her that she might be meeting up with Pete sooner than she had anticipated. *Anytime you feel like lending a hand, buddy, feel free to contribute.* Something tickled the palm of her hand, which was still tied up behind her back. She turned, expecting to see a mouse or something, but saw nothing. Was that Pete letting her know he was there?

CHAPTER TWENTY-ONE

Tony heaved a frustrated sigh when he sat down at the kitchen table. Carol Lang placed a cup of coffee in front of him and rested a hand on his shoulder. "We'll find her soon, love," she said, sitting down beside him.

Tony gave her a brief smile, but then shot out of his chair. "My God—Charlie! Has anyone thought to ring the hospital to see how she is?"

"Sit down. It's all taken care of; don't worry. Jade and Tom are with her," Sam informed him. "They're aware of the situation with Lorne, but they're not going to tell Charlie anything. As far as she knows, her mother is tucked up in bed with a fever."

Tony slumped back into the chair, which creaked under the sudden movement. He hadn't told Sam everything he'd seen at the warehouse. What was there to tell him really, anyway, except that the place stank of sex?

"So what's next, Tony?" Sam asked. His hands were squeezing the life out of his mug.

"I'm not sure, really. Weir and Taylor are going to do some asking around for me, but I don't hold out much hope of them finding anything. I'm wondering if Sean Roberts would be willing to question Angela North for us—is it worth asking him?"

Sam nodded. "What have we got to lose from asking him? She's in custody, anyway."

Tony left the table and dashed into the lounge to ring Roberts. "Sean, it's Tony." He explained what had happened to Lorne and North's part in it, and then asked, "Any chance you can question the wife for me? She looked pretty shaken up, and it's obvious her husband beats her, but she still might know more than she's letting on. Maybe they have a holiday home somewhere or something like that; he might use that to hide Lorne."

"I'll question her myself once I've located her and get back to you. And Tony?"

"Yep?"

"Lorne will come out of this unscathed—she usually does. Have faith in her abilities—and Katy's, for that matter. They're both strong women," Sean said quietly.

"I know you're right, Sean. It doesn't make it any easier or less worrying, though. Speak to you soon, hopefully."

Tony hung up and went back through to the kitchen to find Carol sitting at the table with her eyes closed, rocking back and forth in her chair. Tony gave Sam a questioning look. Sam shrugged his shoulders.

"I see," Lang said after a few more rocks.

"What is it, Carol? What do you see?" Tony asked anxiously.

"Pete's coming through again. He's worried about Lorne..." Carol said before drifting off again.

Tony's patience was being tested to the maximum. However, he knew from past experience that he would have to wait until Carol had finished conversing with the spirits before he found out any information.

"Thank you. Right, Pete said two men have Lorne, Katy, and another woman tied up in the back of some kind of van. He doesn't know in which direction they're heading, but he says that Lorne is remaining strong despite everything."

"Christ, that's bloody cryptic. Despite what?" Tony asked the psychic.

Carol's eyes rose to the ceiling. "That's all he said. We need to locate that van, Tony."

"It's not that simple, Carol. Without a registration number or rough idea of location, the task will be impossible. Have you any idea how many vans are travelling around the London area at any given time? Thousands!"

"Is Pete still here?" Sam asked tentatively, as if he felt foolish asking such a stupid question.

Carol shook her head. "He's gone back to be with Lorne. He'll watch over her, like he always has in the past."

Tony exhaled a short, sharp breath. "That's good to know, at least. Are you sure there's nothing else? Can you visualise the surrounding area, any significant landmarks to help us?"

"I'm sorry, Tony, I wish there was."

The room remained silent for the next few minutes until the phone rang in the lounge. Tony ran through and answered it. "Sean?"

"Sorry, mate. Is Lorne there?"

"Who is this?" Tony snapped at the caller.

"It's Derek Croft. Just get her on the phone, big man. I've got some heavy news for her."

"I'll pass on a message. What's up?" Tony asked, not wishing to tell anyone else that Lorne was missing.

"Lorne or no one," Croft insisted.

Tony picked up the excitement in Croft's voice. "Croft, she ain't here. You can tell me your news and I'll see that she gets it."

"Okay, I guess you are *partners*. My snitch called me to say another shipment of girls is due in today."

"Shit! Where? When?" Tony slammed his clenched fist against his thigh.

"Here's the thing: they're coming in by ship again. It's due to dock at Herne Bay around six o'clock this evening. It's discreet there. Obviously far enough away from the customs at Folkstone."

"Fuck! That's two hours from now. Do you know how many are on board? Crew and girls?"

"Are you kidding me? Do you think my snitches go into details like that? Either you work with what I give you, or I'll find someone else willing to trust my contacts."

"All right, all right, keep your bloody hair on. Thanks for the information. How're the injuries coming along?" Tony wasn't that concerned, but he thought he'd better ask to keep the journalist on his side.

"Actually, the doc's pretty pleased with my progress, and there's even talk of me getting out of here tonight. Might even give me the all clear on his rounds this evening. Hey, I might even make it in time to see you and Lorne bring down the bad guys." He laughed, but Tony didn't. "You're supposed to give me some reaction there, bud. Is there something you're not telling me?"

"I wasn't going to say anything, but…the so-called bad guys have abducted Lorne."

"What the fuck? When?" Croft suddenly sounded agitated, and Tony could hear the sound of what appeared to be bed springs squeaking on the other end of the line.

"A few hours ago. What are you doing?" Tony demanded.

"I'm getting dressed. What do you think I'm doing, playing with my snake?"

Tony grinned and shook his head. "I don't suppose I can talk you out of leaving the hospital, can I?"

"Nope. Where do you want to meet? At the harbour?"

"I guess. It's about an hour from here. Thanks for this, Croft," Tony said. He meant it, too. There were not many folks who would leave their sickbed in hospital to help out a fellow human being, especially one they barely knew. But then, the person in need was someone special who tended to bring out the good in people. Tony wondered if Lorne would be able to work her people skills magic on the men holding her. Then he chastised himself for thinking such a dumb thought.

"No worries. I'll ring a friend to pick me up."

"No, don't do that. I don't want anyone else involved in this."

"I can understand that, but you're forgetting one thing, big man: I'm carless right now."

"Shit, of course you are. Can you get a taxi to a friend's house and maybe borrow their car? That would be better."

"Yeah, makes sense. You better give me your mobile number just in case."

Tony gave Croft his number and then hung up. He walked back into the kitchen to find Sam and Carol looking up at him expectantly. "It was Croft. There's another shipment coming in today."

"Whoa! Hang on a minute—I know that look. You can't possibly be thinking of going down there, Tony. What about Lorne?" Sam asked, frowning.

Tony sat down heavily in the chair alongside him. "I'm not deserting Lorne, Sam—far from it. At the moment she's in a van on the move to who knows where. What if she's actually on her way to the port? If the tables were turned, I know Lorne would follow the leads that came her way. I have to do the same. You understand that, don't you?"

Reluctantly, Sam nodded. "Of course. I'll stay here and hope that either Sean or your pals at MI5 get in touch with fresh information. You get off now, son."

Tony rose, gently squeezed Sam's left shoulder, and patted Henry on the head. "I have a few quick chores to see to around here first. Sam, can you take care of the pups' feeding times? I'll go and feed the dogs in the kennels. I know it's a bit early, but there's no telling what time I'll get back." *Or if I'll get back.*

CHAPTER TWENTY-TWO

Carol volunteered to exercise the dogs while Tony filled up their food and water bowls. Once the chores were completed, he rushed upstairs to the bedroom to change into an all-black outfit—'A covert operation necessity' as MI6 agents liked to call it.

With Sam and Carol's good wishes, Tony set off in the van—hardly the most conspicuous vehicle he could conjure up, but it would have to do. The weather had turned dull and drizzly, so he put the heater on to get a blast of warm air. It was unusual for him to feel the cold; he shivered away the ominous feeling.

He parked outside the port and scanned the area for Croft. Twenty feet in front of him, a red sports car flashed its lights. It had to be Croft. He couldn't help but feel annoyed that the journalist had turned up in a car that would draw attention rather than deflect it. *Dipshit!*

Tony glanced around in all directions to see if anyone was nearby; they weren't. He pulled the van out of its space and came to a stop next to Croft. Croft eased the window down on the sports car and smiled at him. "Get in," Tony said.

He watched the journalist gingerly get out of his vehicle and hobble around the back of the van. Tony leaned across and pushed the passenger's door open.

"Is this a vehicle left over from your days in Her Majesty's Secret Service?"

Tony shook his head at the wisecrack. "How long have you been here?"

"About a minute or so before you turned up. What's the plan?" Croft asked, his eyes darting around nervously.

"I thought you would have a plan up your sleeve."

Croft glared at him. "You're kidding, right?"

"Yeah, I'm kidding." Tony glanced down at the clock on the dashboard. "It's ten minutes to six now; I reckon we should get into position on foot. Are you up to that?"

"I am; are you? I wouldn't want that false leg of yours dropping off before we reached the dock."

"Ha ha! You just concentrate on getting yourself there in one piece and leave me to do the same. Any other information before we go?"

"Such as?" Croft asked, frowning.

"Such as do we know how the girls are going to be transported once they arrive on the dock, bearing in mind it's broad daylight still?"

"Good point." Croft craned his neck to look up at the sky. "Dusk is setting in and it'll be dark in an hour or so, my guess is they'll move the girls then. Like I said, my informant gives me snippets, that's all."

They left the van parked a few feet from Croft's vehicle and walked toward the dock. Croft pointed out to sea. "Could that be it?"

"It could be. We better take cover soon." Tony pointed at a couple of large skips full of building rubbish. "We'll hide behind them. That way, we'll have a clear view of the dock. Damn, I should have brought my binoculars with me."

"Out of practice, old man?" Croft laughed. He placed a hand in the inside pocket of his jacket and extracted a tiny pair of binoculars, the kind you get at an opera house or theatre.

"Great—small, but handy nevertheless." Tony pointed the binoculars out to sea. The name of the ship had worn off slightly, and it was hard to make out. "Looks like two crewmembers on board, as far as I can see. No, wait—there's a third one just appeared."

Croft eagerly snatched the glasses out of Tony's grasp. "There might be more crew downstairs, who knows. They don't seem in a rush to come ashore."

"Probably waiting for nightfall," Tony said. He searched the area and glimpsed a white van waiting along the quayside. Three men on the ship, one in the van—that made four. They were outnumbered two to one. Not great odds. Plus, there was no telling if these men would be armed or not; the likelihood was they would be. Tony reached in his pocket for his mobile and rang a number. "Weir? I'm down at Herne Bay Marina. Got my eye on a boat coming in that could have a connection to our case. The thing is, we're outnumbered and weaponless. Any chance you can give us a hand down here?"

"Who's *we*?" Weir asked, suspicion edging his voice.

"Croft. He's an investigative journalist that Lorne and I have been working with. I'm working off his information."

Weir snorted. "And you trust this guy? A journo?"

"Yep, he's come up with the goods thus far. Even landed up in hospital for his trouble. So? How are you fixed?"

"As it happens, Taylor and I were just about to call it a day. Rather than go home to be with our loving wives, I'm sure we'd be willing to help out a mate again."

"Thanks, mate. See you soon."

Tony hung up and heard Croft exhale. "Something wrong?"

"Not at all. The opposite, actually. I'm glad you called for reinforcements. I didn't really fancy tackling those guys alone. Let's face it: neither of us are in good enough shape to put up a fight."

Offended, Tony replied sharply, "Huh! You speak for yourself. I'm in excellent shape."

"No offence, man, but your leg seems to drop off at will."

"Piss off, Croft. I'll be sure to hang on to it. I wouldn't want you screaming the place down, would I?" Tony watched the smile slip from the journalist's face and mentally stroked the air with his finger, a habit he'd picked up from his wife. *God, I miss you, Lorne.*

For the next thirty minutes, they watched the ship bob up and down just inside the harbour walls. Then, as darkness spread around them, the ship slowly ventured closer to shore.

Croft frantically glanced over his shoulder. "I wish your mates would get a move on."

"You talking about us?" a voice said from the other side of the skip.

"Shit! Give a guy a fucking heart attack, why don't ya!"

Tony laughed as Weir and Taylor came into view. He briefly introduced them to Croft, and then they all focused on the ship. Tony looked through the binoculars. He saw one man moving to the rear and another holding one of the ropes at the front. "I'm still thinking there's only three aboard."

Weir pointed at the van. The driver got out and paced up and down on the edge of the harbour. The guys at the front threw him the rope, which he attached to a concrete post before he moved to the rear and did the same with another rope. The driver climbed aboard the forty-foot ship and high-fived the three men. They shared a joke or two before they all disappeared down below.

"How do you want to play this, Tony? Attack now, or wait until the cargo has been unloaded?"

"I think we should sit tight and wait. Why don't you two try and get a little closer while they're down below?" he said to Taylor and Weir.

They nodded. Crouching, they ran forward and dipped behind a tiny wooden hut.

"Why didn't we do that?" Croft mumbled.

"Because..." Tony replied, kicking himself for having the same thought.

"Yeah, because...?"

"They've got weapons, idiot. We haven't. Now stop whining. Sssh!" Tony said urgently as the four men appeared on deck again. They formed a line between the edge of the boat and what Tony presumed was the hold door. The driver hopped down and opened the rear van doors. A stream of young terrified girls were led off the ship and into the back of the van. The whole process took a matter of minutes.

"What happens now?" Croft asked, shuffling forward to stretch his stiff legs and accidentally kicking a nearby bottle over.

"Shit!" Tony said under his breath as the driver looked their way.

Sensing trouble, the three men on board chattered nervously. When the captain shouted orders to set sail, the driver swore at him. "You can't fucking leave me to deal with this shit."

The captain possibly fearing his escape would be hampered, reluctantly ordered his two men ashore to help load the girls into the van. Tony could see that they all had guns.

Weir gave Tony the thumbs-up. Then all hell broke loose. Amid the shooting, the girls screaming echoed from the van.

Weir and Taylor were cautious not to fire near the van, but the driver was tucked behind the door for safety. Instead, they aimed most of their bullets at the captain and his two crewmen. The crew, now back on the ship were crouched, firing at will in their direction, forcing Tony and Croft to take cover.

Tony hated feeling inadequate. He should have asked Weir if he had a backup weapon he could have used, but the thought hadn't crossed his mind before.

"Do something! We can't sit it out here," Croft said, looking scared.

"That's just what we're going to have to do. If you hadn't alerted them to us being here, we wouldn't be in this shit now. Tell you what—why don't you just keep your fucking mouth shut?"

Tony looked around him and saw a large wooden pole lying beside the skip. He picked it up and ran around the skip, heading for the van. If he could take on the driver, it would help. He reached the side of the van and crept toward the back, where the driver was situated. His foot hit a rock, and he looked down. Suddenly the driver was standing in front of him, his gun aimed at his head.

"Drop it!" the driver snarled and moved closer to him.

Reluctantly, Tony threw the pole aside. He waited for the man to get closer. Then, catching the man unaware, he charged him like a raging bull. The man grunted when Tony rammed his head into the man's stomach, but he didn't let go of the gun, as Tony had expected. They fought, Tony's fists connected with the man's face and upper body several times. A gun went off close by. Tony froze when he realised he'd been hit.

CHAPTER TWENTY-THREE

The balding man, who stood a good four inches taller than him, gave Tony a puzzled look. Seizing the opportunity to pounce on the man's confused state Tony issued a punch to the man's windpipe, and the gun flew out of his hand and slid under the van. Tony was the first to react. He retrieved the gun and told the man to put his hands on his head. When he did, Tony grabbed the man and smashed him against the side of the van.

The man's muffled voice said, "But…I shot you."

Tony laughed. "You hit my fake leg, arsehole." Then he called out to Weir and Taylor, "I've got the driver."

Detecting Tony's distraction, the driver kicked out at Tony's fake leg. The leg gave way beneath him, and the gun bounced across the concrete, far enough away that neither man could reach it. The driver jumped on top of Tony, his hands clasped around Tony's throat. The man was stronger than he looked, and Tony struggled for breath. Then another shot rang out a few feet from them. The man's grip loosened and he collapsed on Tony's chest. Tony heaved the man off him to see Croft holding the gun.

"Do you mind pointing that thing the other way in case it goes off again?" Tony said, scrambling to his feet.

He took the gun from Croft's extended shaking hand. "I just killed a man," Croft said numbly.

"You'll get over it. Look at it this way: he was a dirtbag, and the world will be a better place without him," Tony assured him, amused by his reaction.

He switched back into agent mode and peered around the edge of the van's rear door at the ship. The men firing at Weir and Taylor were in plain sight; it would be easy for him to take them out. They wouldn't be expecting any bullets to be fired from his location. He aimed the gun and fired off four shots. The two shooters went down, which left only the captain of the vessel to deal with. Tony saw Weir and Taylor run up to the ship and climb aboard. He'd let them deal with the captain. Within seconds, two more shots sounded in the night air.

Croft nudged Tony in the ribs. He turned around to see the girls clinging to each other in the back of the van. All of them looked— and probably were—underage, and much too young for the life they had been destined to lead. He smiled and felt sick to the stomach. A few of them gave a brief smile in response, but most of them just stared at him in bewilderment.

"You're safe now, believe me." Tony closed the van doors gently and said to Croft, "I'm just going to make a call."

He stepped away from the van and dialled a number. "Sean, it's Tony. Sorry to trouble you out of office hours, but—"

"Have you found them?"

Tony sighed heavily. "Not yet, I'm still working on that. I've just rescued another shipment of girls. Any chance your lot can come and collect them? Oh, and there are three dead men to deal with, too."

"What? How the fuck did that happen, Tony?"

"Umm...Croft called me with some information that the girls were coming in by boat. I arranged for two mates from MI5 to be on standby in case I needed them. Well, one thing led to another, and there was a little shootout. Nothing major."

"Nothing major! Fucking hell, Tony. I'll get a crew down there now. What state are the girls in and how many are there?"

"As expected, they're petrified. Can you arrange for some female officers to attend? I think it would help. The girls' clothes look as though they could do with replacing, so a change of clothes would help, as well."

"Yeah, first things first, though: let's get them checked over and in a warm place. Despite my anger, I appreciate what you've done, Tony. Oh, by the way, I was going to ring you after I'd had dinner."

"With some news, I hope?"

"Angela North is still maintaining that she had nothing to do with her husband's new business, and to be honest, I'm inclined to believe her. I did some digging on Roger North, and apparently he got the sack from his job in the city about six weeks ago. When I asked his wife about it, it was obvious she had no idea. He'd been sticking to his routine of staying in London during the week and going home at the weekend to be with her and his kid. He's clearly got another woman on the side, or he's been dipping his wick at one of his many brothels."

"Sick bastard! I'm going to enjoy beating the crap out of him when I catch up with him, especially if he's laid a finger on either Lorne or Katy."

"Hang on, there's more. This might be significant to you. Angela suddenly remembered that North owns a boat—a cruiser. It's moored at Ramsgate Marina. If you have nothing else, it's worth a try."

"If that's the best we can come up with, then I'll give it a shot. Ramsgate, I reckon that's about a fifty minutes to an hour from here. My mates are still with me; I'm sure I can persuade them to tag along. Thanks, Sean, I'll let you know how we get on. I'll leave Croft here with the girls—or would you rather we moved them elsewhere, just in case?" Tony asked, searching the area for any sign of bystanders the shootout might have attracted.

"I'll get a response team there immediately. Leave Croft there. Then go and find my sergeant and your wife," Sean ordered.

Tony hung up and told Croft to stay put with the girls until the coppers arrived. The journalist wasn't keen on the idea, but agreed to do it all the same.

Weir and Taylor walked over to join them and congratulated Tony on his part in the gun battle. "It was nothing. Glad I remembered which way to point the gun." They all laughed. "Right, now for the next stage in this scenario. I've just been informed that North has a boat moored about an hour from here. I was thinking that maybe you guys would come with me for moral support?"

"Moral support or another shootout?" Weir smiled.

"Whichever. Can we get going, maybe take your car?"

"That's a given, considering your heap up the road. We spotted it when we pulled up, hardly a covert operation vehicle, mate, is it?" Taylor ribbed him.

"Yeah, I know, get all the jibes over and done with now. Lorne got run off the road the other day by this mob and our car is in the workshop. It was either that thing or nothing."

CHAPTER TWENTY-FOUR

Leaving a dejected Croft behind, Tony and the two agents drove to Ramsgate. En route, Tony rang Lorne's father to apprise him of the situation.

"Tony, did everything go all right?" Sam asked, sounding pleased to hear from him.

"So-so, Sam. I'll fill you in on the details later. I heard back from Sean. We are—that's Weir, Taylor, and me— on our way to Ramsgate. It could be a false alarm we're chasing up, but Sean found out from North's wife that he has a boat moored there. I can't see him taking Lorne to any of his brothels, can you?"

"No, I can't. That's great news... Hold on a second."

After several moments passed without Sam's return Tony began to worry "Sam? Are you there?"

"Sorry, Tony. Listen, Carol has just had one of her visions. You could be on to something."

"What did she see?" Tony asked as his adrenaline surged.

"She saw a large cruiser and a sheep. She couldn't figure out why a sheep would be on a boat, but it fits now, if you think about it."

"That's amazing. Yes, a ram will fit in there nicely. Tell Carol thanks, and keep your fingers crossed that we're on the right track. I'll be in touch when I can. Any news on Charlie?"

"I rang the hospital about half an hour ago—there's no change. She's keeping her spirits up, though, so that's a blessing. I apologised for us not being there, and she's fine with that. Jade has taken the two boys in to see her this evening."

Tony smiled at the thought of Jade's children giving the nurses the run-around. "Let's hope bringing her mum home safe and sound will have a positive effect on her. I'll ring you later."

After hanging up, Tony rested his head back against the headrest and contemplated what lay ahead of them if they managed to locate North and his boat at the marina. He felt an unexpected pain in his chest when Lorne's beautiful face drifted into his mind. *Never doubt how much I love you, Lorne. Stay positive. I'm coming to...get you.*

* * *

When they arrived at the marina, all was relatively quiet, except for one boat where a party appeared to be going on.

"That could work to our advantage," Weir said, pointing at the partygoers on board.

Tony nodded in agreement as he got out of the car. The party could mask their movements if the need arose to get aboard North's boat. They left the car in the marina car park and walked along the jetty, trying to act casual and on their way to the party.

Taylor asked Tony, "Any idea of this boat's name?"

Tony shook his head in frustration. "Roberts didn't say, and I forgot to ask."

"Well, there doesn't seem to be a lot of choice around here, anyway," Weir commented, eyeing the few boats moored to the jetty.

"Granted. Why don't we mingle with the punters at the party and ask around—maybe the owner of the boat is an acquaintance of North's," Tony replied, feeling less optimistic that they had come to the right place.

"That's a good idea, except that none of us are dressed up enough to go to a party," Taylor grumbled, looking down at the faded jeans he was wearing.

"Nonsense, it's the done thing to dress down for these things nowadays, isn't it?" Tony said, remembering a remark Lorne had made the week before about how no one appeared to bother getting dressed up to attend film premieres anymore.

Once all three men were aboard the lively cruiser, a young man holding a silver tray approached them. "Would you like a cocktail? If not, grab a bottle of beer from the bar."

"Thanks, we'll do that," Weir said, leading the way through the crowd full of people swaying to the music of the jazz band playing on the bow.

"Keep your eyes peeled for a likely host or hostess," Tony said, squeezing past a scantily clad teenager who turned and looked him up and down with hunger.

"Over there." Taylor pointed at a young man in his early twenties who had a bevy of beauties hanging around him. "I'll go," Taylor volunteered.

Tony and Weir stood at the bar, acting as though they were enjoying themselves. Taylor joined them a few minutes later. He downed a mouthful of lager before informing them, "He said he's not sure what the guy's name is who owns the boat, but a cruiser left the harbour about half an hour ago."

"Great! Did he say how many people were on board?" Tony asked, anxiously wringing his hands together.

"Nope, he was too busy welcoming his guests. If it was North, he timed his getaway perfectly."

"Damn, I don't suppose he knew the name of the boat, did he?" Tony asked, looking out to sea, fear beginning to mount in his belly.

"I didn't ask," Taylor admitted quietly.

Weir raised a hand. "All is not lost. There's a pub back there on the quay. I'll go back and ask the staff if they know North and the name of his boat. Someone around here is bound to know. In the meantime, you two ask around the harbour, see if you can borrow a speed boat or something, just in case."

The three of them weaved their way back through the crowd and split up in different directions once they were on the jetty.

Tony worked his way along the jetty, checking the ignitions of the small craft as he passed on off chance that maybe one of the owners had left the keys there. No such luck. Then an idea struck him. He made his way back to the cruiser where the party was being held and searched around the side of it. *Bingo!* A small dinghy was tied to the cruiser. Something caught his eye inside the boat. Glistening in the lights blazing on the boat was a key hanging in the ignition.

His eyes rose heavenward, and under his breath he thanked Pete.

He whistled to Taylor at the end of the jetty who had just been joined by Weir, the two agents ran to meet him. "I've got a dinghy. What did you find out, Weir?"

"The owner told me the cruiser is called *Wayward Girl.* He also said that he moved a barrel outside about forty minutes ago and saw five people get on the boat before it set off."

"That must have been them. We've got to get after them. We should get in touch with the U.K. Border Agency." Tony's mind was in turmoil. All he wanted to do was get to Lorne as quickly as possible, but he knew he had to put a backup plan into action first.

"I'll do it now," Weir said, patting Tony on the back as he placed the call to the authorities. After a quick conversation, he turned back to Tony. "Let's get in the boat."

They jumped in and started the engine, then looked up to see the host of the party shaking his fist at them. "Get the fuck out of there! I'm calling the police."

Tony waved and gave him the thumbs-up. "That'd be great. Don't worry; we'll return her safely in a couple of hours." He pointed the small craft out to sea. As they rounded the harbour wall, the full weight of the task ahead of them hit Tony. Which way should they go? Once the lights of the harbour faded, only the pitch black of the night lay ahead. "All right, any suggestions?"

"No idea. Can you see any binoculars lying around?" Taylor asked, looking under his seat.

Tony dug the small pair of binoculars out of his pocket he had acquired from Croft and handed them to Taylor, who searched the surrounding darkness. Tony shuddered. The night air out at sea was much colder than inland—or was that him just being fearful for Lorne's safety? Out here in the dark, anything might—and was likely to—happen, if North had his way.

"Nothing yet," Taylor said, "Let's go farther out."

Tony steered the boat in the direction he thought North might have taken and prayed that he was right. After ten minutes of fruitless searching, Taylor suddenly pointed.

"There. I can just make out a faint light."

Tony snatched the glasses from him and looked for himself. Sure enough, far off in the distance was a dim light that could be the boat they were after. It was time to take a gamble on his instinct and get to the boat as fast as was humanly possible. He upped the speed, and Weir and Taylor tipped back and lost their balance in the small craft. *I'm on a mission to rescue the woman I love. All I need now is a box of Milk Tray.* Tony grinned.

* * *

Lorne felt helpless, a feeling that she hadn't experienced often in her life, and she didn't like it one bit. She glanced over at Katy, who looked as though she were going to be sick at any moment. The two men who'd abducted them were at the bow of the boat, and the three girls remained tied up in the stern. They were secured tightly now, with added rope tied around their ankles. The rope had an anchor attached to the other end. Lorne gulped; she could sense a watery ending for all of them. It was imperative that she and Katy work together to get them out of this predicament.

"Katy? Can you hear me?" she whispered.

A groan came from Katy's direction, followed by the sound of someone heaving and vomiting.

Shit! "Katy, what is it? Tell me." Fear and concern rippled in her voice. She stared at her friend.

"Seasickness," Katy managed to say before she vomited a second time. Afterward, she sat back against the side of the boat and hung her head wearily.

Fuck! Bang goes any master plan I might have of getting us out of here alive with Katy unable to count on for support.

She pleaded with Katy, "Hon, listen to me. Take a few deep breaths. I need your help or we're going to die."

Lorne was greeted with silence and wondered if she'd overstepped the mark with her last statement.

Finally Katy coughed, wiped her mouth on the shoulder of her blouse, and pulled her head and shoulders upright. "Since you put it that way, I have little choice in the matter. I'm not sure if I'll be much help, Lorne, but I'm willing to give it a shot."

"That's my girl. Now all we have to do is figure out how to get out of these ropes. Can you move your wrists at all?"

"No. If anything, trying to move them makes the rope rub them sore. What about you?"

"Same here."

A small voice from the corner spoke out, "My hands are not tied tight."

"Really, Jai San? Could you possibly slip one hand out, maybe?"

"I try."

Lorne heard the girl struggle and bang her elbow against the boat several times before she held an arm up in the air.

My God, she did it! "Fantastic, sweetheart. If you hear the men coming, quickly put your arm behind your back and pretend that you're still tied up, okay?"

"Yes, okay. What I do now?" Jai San asked, her eyes wide as saucers.

"Can you try and untie me? Be quiet when you move, though, okay?"

"Okay."

Jai San moved her slight body with agility and scooted behind Lorne's back, careful not to drag the anchor with her. She tugged on the rope for what seemed like hours before managing to loosen it enough for Lorne to slip her hands out. Lorne hugged the girl and then gently pushed her away.

"Go back to where you were. I'll see to Katy." Lorne twisted and moved the three feet or so towards Katy, cautious about not shifting the anchor tied to her feet. Katy winced and drew in a sharp breath when Lorne started to pull on the rope. "I'll be as gentle as I can, hon." The rope appeared to be tightening rather than loosening, until one large tug seemed to do the trick and Katy's hands sprang free. They hugged each other. Lorne quickly returned to her position. Then they waited for their opportunity to arise.

CHAPTER TWENTY-FIVE

The cruiser was about three hundred feet ahead of them now. Tony pulled back on the throttle to slow the dinghy down. "Are you guys ready for this?" he asked Weir and Taylor.

"Yep, armed and ready. Let's take these fuckers out," Taylor said with all the enthusiasm of a kid in a sweet shop.

It took them another ten minutes to catch up with the cruiser. Tony cut the engine and eased the dinghy alongside the craft. Weir stood up at the front and grasped one of the fenders hanging down the side of North's boat. He pulled the dinghy along towards the boarding ladder on the side. The ladder could be their access to the cruiser.

"What the fuck?" a man's voice called out.

Shit! We've been spotted.

Weir fired off a shot. Then Tony heard a familiar voice shout, "Tony, we're in here, at the back of the boat."

"Lorne—she's alive." Tony flew out of his seat and tried to climb up the ladder, but Taylor pulled him back.

"Hold on, mate. Let's take this nice and easy."

"Yeah," agreed Weir, "I'm not sure if I shot the guy or not."

They heard a commotion, a lot of scuffling, and the girls screaming. "No way. I'm getting on there *now*." He shouldered his way past the two agents, climbed the ladder, and jumped aboard the cruiser without considering his own welfare. His one thought was for the safety of his wife. The deck was empty, Tony urged the two agents to hurry up. He turned to face the cabin at the rear and stopped dead. A thickset man was holding a knife at the throat of an Asian girl.

"One step closer, moron, and she goes overboard."

Tony heard Taylor and Weir land on the deck behind him, and one of them muttered, "Shit!"

Tony held up his hands. "There's no need to harm anyone. You can see that you're outnumbered, let the girl go."

"Yeah, I'm full of tricks like that, arsehole. Now, get back in your little boat and fuck off out of here," the man said, pulling his arm tighter around the girl's throat, causing her to choke.

Tony turned back to Weir and Taylor behind him. "Come on, guys, there's not a lot we can do here." His eyes darted off to the side and he mouthed to Weir, "shoot him when I drop". He saw Weir reach a hand around to his back, and then he gave Tony a brief nod of understanding.

Turning back to the bad guy, Tony shrugged. "You've got it, man, I don't want any unnecessary agro." After the final word, he dropped down to the floor as if a lead weight had landed on him from a great height.

Weir took the shot. Blood oozed from the wound between the man's eyes, and he instantly dropped the knife. The girl saw her opportunity to escape and ran toward the agents, screaming. The shot man fell to the deck seemingly in slow motion.

Taylor tore off his jacket and slung it around the girl's shuddering shoulders. "You're safe," he told her as he pushed her gently down on the seat behind them.

She might be, but Lorne and Katy aren't—not with North still on the loose! Tony thought as he and Weir quietly moved toward the cabin. They'd be foolish to think that North hadn't heard the shot, and it was imperative they get to the girls as soon as they possibly could.

But things suddenly changed when they heard a woman's scream and then a large splash. Without further thought, Tony ran forward, but Taylor's voice halted his progress. "Tony, take this." He threw Tony his handgun. Tony caught it and rushed into the wheelhouse. He heard another big splash and realised that Weir had also gone into the sea after whoever had been thrown overboard. That was one less thing to worry about. Tony heard noises behind the cabin door. He pushed it open slowly, and halted when he saw Katy standing naked in front of a grinning North. Tony averted his gaze, blocking out Katy's shapely figure, and focused fully on North. He was playing with the tip of a large blade. Tony moved an inch more and the blade slashed across Katy's upper arm.

"Shit! Don't hurt her!"

"He's pushed Lorne overboard, Tony! Forget about me—go and save her," Katy cried out as blood ran down the length of her arm.

"She's a wise woman, Tony, you should listen to her."

"My colleague is dealing with that matter, North. Let her go." Tony raised the gun and calmly aimed it at North's head. The man's eyes creased and he appeared to be momentarily confused. *Had he expected me to go after Lorne, leaving him to have a clean getaway with Katy?*

He wondered if he made a gesture to Katy she would get his meaning and duck, giving him a free shot at North. Tony widened his eyes and looked to the right, Katy doubled over and Tony fired off the shot. North's reaction was too slow and he fell to the floor. Tony searched the immediate area for a blanket or something to wrap Katy in.

Katy shouted at him, "Go, Tony! Get Lorne—she has an anchor tied to her leg."

"Fuck!" He turned and ran back out onto the deck. "Have you seen her?" he anxiously asked Taylor.

Taylor, who was peering over the side of the boat, looked up at him with an exasperated expression and shook his head.

"I'm going in. North's dead. Katy is safe. Can you look around for a powerful flashlight—something that will throw some light down there?"

"You've got it. Be careful, Tony."

Tony unstrapped his leg—to the horror of Jai San—and dived into the water. It was a good job that some of his physiotherapy had taken place in the pool. He dipped under the water, but the darkness above and below the water made it impossible to make out anything. Within seconds, the area was flooded with light and he spotted Weir and Lorne struggling just below the water's surface, about twenty feet away from him. He swam to help them. His eyes locked onto Lorne's, and the fear he saw there scared him. He pulled Weir away, urging him to get to the surface to refill the air in his lungs. Then he covered Lorne's mouth with his own and released some air between her lips, then pulled away from her and dived down to tackle the anchor around her ankle.

Weir rejoined them and began cutting at the anchor rope with a small blade. With one final tug, the anchor fell away from Lorne's leg. The three of them resurfaced and gasped for air. Taylor threw a life jacket in their direction, and Weir swam to it. He returned and slipped it over Lorne's head and shoulders.

"Oh, Tony, I thought I was a goner," she spluttered in between gasps of breath.

"Hey, it would take a lot more than an anchor to end your life, love." He smiled and kissed her lightly on the lips, then hugged her. The three of them swam around the other side of the boat. They climbed into the dinghy, then up the boarding ladder and onto the deck of the cruiser.

Taylor greeted them with an armful of blankets. "Where's Katy?" Lorne asked breathlessly.

From the entrance to the cabin, a shaky voice replied, "I'm here, Lorne."

Lorne ran to her friend and wrapped her arms around her. "Thank God you're safe."

"Thank God we're both safe. I've never been so scared in all my life." Katy sobbed as the tears flowed freely.

"Yeah, and to think about an hour ago all you were worried about was feeling a bit seasick," Lorne teased as relieved tears ran down her ice-cold cheeks.

Weir started up the cruiser and headed back to port. Tony watched the three girls cling to each other as they sat on the bench at the bow. His own thoughts were filled with how much he loved his wife and how he was going to prove it to her when he returned home.

Sean Roberts was waiting for them when they docked. He greeted them with relieved hugs for Lorne and Katy and firm handshakes for Tony and the two agents.

"What happened to the girls?" Tony asked as the group made their way back to their respective vehicles.

"They'll be taken care of. The Border Patrol came and took them away. They're being checked out at the hospital and then will be transferred to a secure home. Then they'll be on their way back home to their families, thanks to you guys," Sean told them with a grateful smile.

"Sean, when we were at the warehouse, North received a call from someone. By his reaction and tone of voice, I would say it was from someone higher up in the chain of command," Lorne said.

Sean Roberts looked puzzled. "You mean North wasn't the top man in all of this?"

Lorne shook her head. "I don't think so."

"You guys get off to the hospital. Leave me to do some more digging, and I'll get back to you in a day or two."

EPILOGUE

Over the course of the following week, Lorne received news that Charlie had regained the use of her legs—not fully, but it was a start. The doctor told her that Charlie's recovery would be slow and that she would need a few months of intensive physiotherapy before she could lead a normal teenager's life again. But the prognosis was good—that was the main thing, despite Lorne's initial misgivings.

Katy had been recalled to the Met after Sean had interviewed the suspect who had made the ridiculous accusation against her. Sean had persuaded the suspect with the vague threat that it would be in his best interests if he dropped the charges. The suspect had seen the error of his ways and Katy had been reinstated to DS within twenty-four hours. Lorne was relieved; after careful consideration, she'd realised that the P.I. business didn't have enough work to warrant Katy joining the team just yet. She also knew it was imperative that Katy get back to work as soon as possible for her own peace of mind after the trauma North had subjected her to.

Lorne's father had caused her some concern throughout the week. She had a feeling that he'd been putting on a brave face and wasn't a hundred percent fit. Against his wishes, she had asked the doctor to pay her father a visit. The doctor had ordered bed rest, but, Sam being Sam, had brushed off the doctor's advice. Nevertheless, Lorne had insisted her father take it easy that week and just potter around the house instead of helping to clear up in the kennels after the boarders. Her father had reluctantly agreed.

Tony hadn't left her side all week, which, while she found it nice to be the centre of attention, she soon felt rather suffocated. An awkward incident occurred where she backed into him in one of the kennels and the poop she'd been shovelling ended up in her wellies, she ended up blowing her top at him.

On Friday morning of the following week, the phone rang. Lorne answered.

"Hello?"

"Lorne, it's Sean."

"Well, you took your time getting back to me. What have you found out—anything?"

"I'll pick you up in an hour." He hung up abruptly.

Lorne stared at the phone after he'd hung up.

True to his word, Sean arrived at the house an hour later with Katy.

"Hey, you two! What the hell is going on?"

Sean smiled and winked at her. "Get your shoes and your coat. I'd like you and Tony to join us."

Perplexed, she asked, "Where? Why?"

Katy tutted. "Just get your coat and stop asking bloody questions for once in your life."

Suitably reprimanded she raced around getting ready, a buzz of excitement beginning to build inside. "Tony, get a move on," she called upstairs five minutes later. "Will you be okay, Dad?"

Her father was sitting at the kitchen table, petting Henry beside him. He gave her a weary smile and waved a hand in front of him. "You go, I'll be fine here with the boy."

Lorne saw Sean and her father exchange knowing winks. *Hmm...what the dickens is going on? Dad obviously knows something.*

Lorne and Tony sat in the back of Sean's Lexus, while Katy rode up front with him. They drove through the country lanes in virtual silence until they pulled up outside a familiar mansion house.

"I'm confused. What are we doing here, Sean?"

"You'll see."

He got out of the car and the rest of them followed him up to the front door. A man in a smart black suit opened the door. The man appeared to be as confused as Lorne to see them all standing on his doorstep.

"Mind if we come in?" Sean demanded, rather than asked.

"What's the meaning of this? Who are you?"

Sean introduced himself and Katy, then he turned to Lorne and Tony and said, "Mr. and Mrs. Warner have been helping us with a case—they're private investigators."

The man's face drained of all colour and he stepped back. Lorne expected the group to be let in, but the man reached behind the door and pulled out a shotgun.

"There's no need for that, Mr. Wallace. All we want to do is come in for a little chat."

"Fuck off. Get off my property." He snarled, showing his true colours.

Lorne was still at a loss as to why they were there. However, Sean's next words dropped a bombshell.

"Come on, Wallace, the game is up. You've been implicated in this case up to your scrawny neck. Stop being an idiot and put the gun down."

Wallace was having none of it. He cocked the gun and took aim. "You're fucking crazy. I haven't got a clue what you're talking about."

"Is that so?" Sean said. "Then why the gun? Looks like a sign of guilt to me. There's a team of armed officers on their way here right now. Let's talk about this calmly…"

Before he could continue, they heard a loud noise and broken pieces of porcelain dropped on the step in front of them, Wallace tumbled to the ground. Sean managed to grab the barrel of the gun before it hit the floor and they all breathed a sigh of relief. In the doorway stood a trembling Mai Lin, her hands on either side of her face, huge tears dripping onto her cheeks.

Lorne rushed to comfort her and guided her through to the lounge, where Natasha was sitting with Timmy the dog. Natasha jumped out of her seat when they walked in.

"Lorne? What in God's name is going on here?"

"Natasha, I'm as much in the dark as you are. I'm sure all will be revealed in a moment or two." Lorne looked over her shoulder to see Tony and Sean dragging Jason Wallace into the room.

"Jason!" Natasha rushed to her husband's side. She ran her hand over his handsome face and screeched, "What have you done to him?"

"He raped me," Mai Lin's quiet voice said from the corner.

Natasha stood up and her mouth fell open. Her gaze searched those of the group standing in front of her. She shook her head. "No, not Jason. He…he wouldn't."

Lorne stepped forward and gently guided Natasha over to the sofa. Natasha stared at her as she sat down. Lorne joined her on the sofa and held Natasha's hand in her lap and nodded. "Natasha, I'm sure that's not all Jason has done. Am I right, Sean?"

He nodded his head slowly. "I believe we have you to thank for highlighting this awful situation, Mrs. Wallace."

"I don't understand. Please, tell me what my husband has been up to."

Lorne ran through what had happened since Natasha had put them on the trail of the agency. Halfway through the story, Natasha held up a hand to stop Lorne. She looked over at Mai Lin and invited the young woman to sit down beside her. Mai Lin hesitantly did as her employer instructed. Natasha gripped the young woman's hand as fresh tears ran down both of their faces.

It was obvious to the group that Natasha Wallace had nothing to do with her husband's secret business. She was clearly appalled by what she was hearing. When Lorne continued, implicating Roger North in the business, as well, Natasha exclaimed, "My God! I can't believe it."

Jason Wallace stirred in the armchair near the door. Before anyone could stop her, Natasha sprinted across the room and slapped her husband around the face and head, sobbing and shouting with every blow she made, until, finally exhausted, she sank to her knees on the carpet beside him. "How could you?"

Jason Wallace numbly stared down at her and said nothing. What could he say? He was led away by two officers.

Mai Lin was taken into protective custody with the other girls. The authorities were already in the process of sorting out the necessary paperwork to send them back home to their native countries.

Lorne asked Natasha if she wanted to call a relative to be with her. Natasha thanked her for her kindness and then left the room to pack a bag so that she could go and stay with her sister.

Sean and Katy dropped Lorne and Tony back home. During the journey, Sean told them that Tara Small had finally come forward with a list of all the people involved in the trafficking ring. Wallace was the first one to be arrested. They had organised simultaneous raids on ten other properties. At least the organisers of this operation would be behind bars for years and unable to ship any more girls in to the country.

Getting out of the car, their mood was a buoyant one. "I have to hand it to Mai Lin, it took courage to whack Wallace over the head with a Ming vase like that," Lorne said.

The group laughed behind her as she pushed open the back door to the house. Before stepping in through the door, she paused with her hand on the handle and stared.

Tony ran into the back of her. "Get a move on, girl, I'm gasping for a cuppa."

"Tony!" she cried out and fell against the door.

Her husband pushed past her and into the kitchen, where he found Lorne's father draped across the kitchen table. He rushed to her father's aid, but it was too late.

"No!" Lorne cried out from the doorway before her legs gave way beneath her.

Katy fell down beside her and gathered Lorne in her arms. She rocked Lorne back and forth and smoothed a hand over her hair. "I'm so sorry, Lorne."

Lorne watched as Tony and Sean sat her father up and checked his wrist and neck for a pulse, but Lorne knew it would be a pointless exercise—they wouldn't find one.

Her eyes rose to the ceiling. *Pete, come and collect him for me. Make sure he's reunited with Mum soon.*

Then she slowly made her way into the lounge, picked up the phone to ring her sister. She knew Jade would take the news badly and pushed her own emotions aside to cope with her sister's grief.

"Jade, it's me. Are you sitting down?"

"What? What is it? Just tell me, is it Charlie, has she had a relapse?"

Lorne collapsed into the sofa feeling numb. "It's you and me girl."

"What do you..." Jade's voice trailed off. Lorne heard her sister expel a breath as she sat down heavily. "It's dad, isn't it?"

"He's gone, love."

The End

ABOUT THE AUTHOR

New York Times, USA Today, Amazon Top 20 bestselling author, iBooks top 5 bestselling and #2 bestselling author on Barnes and Noble. I am a British author who moved to France in 2002, and that's when I turned my hobby into a career.
I share my home with two crazy dogs that like nothing better than to drag their masterful leader (that's me) around the village.
When I'm not pounding the keys of my computer keyboard I enjoy DIY, reading, gardening and painting.

Made in the USA
Lexington, KY
09 October 2016